VIEW TO THE NORTH

EDITH KONECKY

HAMILTON STONE EDITIONS

Published in the United States by Hamilton Stone Editions,
New Jersey.

Library of Congress Cataloging-in-Publication Data

Konecky, Edith
View to the North/Edith Konecky
p.cm.
ISBN 0-9714873-3-2 (alk.paper)
1. Adult children of aging parents—Fiction. 2. Parent and
adult child—Fiction. 3. Fathers and daughters—Fiction. 4.
Middle-aged women—Fiction. 5. Loss (psychology)—
Fiction. 6. Bisexual women—Fiction. 7. Florida—Fiction.
I. Title.

PS3561.0457V54.2004
813'.54—dc22
2004002358

Manufactured in the United States of America

Cover design by Joshua Konecky

VIEW TO THE NORTH

Also by Edith Konecky

Allegra Maud Goldman
A Place at the Table
Past Sorrows and Coming Attractions

VIEW TO THE NORTH

As you get older, it gets colder.
You see through things.
I'm looking through the trees,

Their torn and thinning leaves,
to where chill blue water
is roughened by wind.

Day by day the scene opens,
enlarges, rips of space
appear where full branches

used to snug the view.
Soon it will be wide, stripped,
entirely unobstructed:

I'll see right through
the twining waves, to
the white horizon, to the place

where the North begins.
Magnificent! I'll be thinking
While my eyeballs freeze.

May Swenson

ONE (Now)

Coming up out of sleep is like thrashing out of a swamp overhung with torn and tangled vines of dreams. When I break through, the first thing I see is the cat, sitting on the windowsill looking at the view, her tail swishing in thought, or whatever it is that goes on in cats' heads. Maybe, like me, she's wondering what became of that vivid slope of trees that so recently flared and sputtered into this dun winter landscape. Do cats think in color? The cat herself, a calico, is a fanciful child's crayon drawing, snowy-breasted, orange, black, with scribbles here and there among the orange, and eyes the green of that child's favorite marble, the one he'd never dream of swapping.

The cat's name is Minnie and she's useful. Because of her, I punch occasional holes in the silence by pretending to talk to her, though I am usually talking to myself. Now, seeing that I'm awake, she jumps onto the bed and sits on my stomach, purring. Through the window, I can see a great cloudbank moving in to cover the thin morning sun, turning the sky leaden. It isn't going to be a good day. I feel that familiar small nibbling fear. "We could go back to New York," I tell the cat, who's rubbing her cheek against my hand, purring with morning love. New York is home. I grew up there, my friends are there, Angie is there. Some-where.

I dreamt of Angie. I often do. In the dream, she was a bright, feisty beagle prancing down a broad street with a fish in her mouth, proudly bringing it home. But it was a dangerous street and the dog, Angie, was run over by a house while I, the dreamer, whoever I was, watched in horror. The house moved on and the dog, Angie, lay there, her legs crushed. The dreamer checked an impulse to run and save her. Instead, with a sickening feeling that was more memory than present emotion, a feeling of impotence and guilt, I changed the dream.

"No," I tell Minnie, "we're not ready to go back."

We're here for the silences, but mostly to get away from Angie. The silences are the white spaces in which I'm able to listen to myself, and they're also the spaces in which I hope I'm mending. Still, I feel the familiar pain of missing Angie. Will it never stop?

There was so much in that short dream. It was like one of those birthday party grab bags of childhood, with ribbons rayed out, one for each child. You pulled your ribbon and drew out your surprise dime-store toy. The dream had a lot of ribbons, each leading to its carefully packaged revelation; I have only to slide them forth one by one. I know that the dream contained Angie's accident all mixed up with the time my first dog, Smokey, was run over when I was eight years old and inconsolable. My mother slept in my room that night, an unprecedented acknowledgment of the power of a child's grief.

I lift the cat off my stomach and slide out of bed. During my hectic night, I awoke with four lines in my head that may be the beginning of a new poem, and I stumbled to the typewriter to get them down. Now I'm eager to get back to my desk to see if they're as compelling in the cold light of this cold day as they were in the night and, if so, where they will take me.

I'm brushing my teeth when, for the first time in two days, the phone rings. I spit and quickly rinse. The last call was from Jed, in Boston, reminding me to send money for books and supplies. Now it's my mother, calling from Florida.

"What's wrong?" I ask. My mother calls at ten every Sunday morning. This is Friday.

"It's Daddy," she says, her voice tight. "He's in the hospital. Can you come?"

"Of course. What is it?"

I hear her take a deep breath. "He didn't feel well during the night," she says, "so early this morning we went to the hospital. Dr. Greenberg put him right in intensive care. His heart was failing."

"What do you mean?"

"What do you mean what do I mean? Failing. Not doing what a heart is supposed to do. They're trying out a pacemaker, externally. If it works, they'll implant it."

I feel that rush of adrenaline. "I'll check connections and make arrangements," I say.

"Arrangements? The cat?" She has never been sympathetic to my cat.

"I'll be there as early as possible tomorrow. I'll call you later."

We hang up and I stand, shivering, dying for a cigarette. Dying. If my father is dying, how can I not have a cigarette? It's been seven weeks since the last one, seven weeks during which I've done almost no work. Not smoking is a full time job. Inspiration won't come unless sucked through that lethal straw, that pacifier. Tentative as it was, last night felt like a tiny breakthrough, those four lines. The poem was, or will be, about memory running forward in time instead of backward, and anticipation backward rather than forward. I almost have the metaphor.

I dial Blanche's number. Blanche is a sculptor friend who lives nearby. We have a mutual cat-sitting arrangement. Her phone rings and rings. It's much too early to call anyone, especially Blanche who often works through the night. At last, she picks up and moans.

"I'm sorry, Blanche. Emergency. My father is dying. Maybe."

"Bring her." No word-waster she.

"I don't know how long . . . "

"I'm not going anywhere except back to sleep. Sorry about your father. Hope it's a false alarm."

I find the number for Delta. A live, untaped voice, eager to please, assures me that I can easily make the two PM snack flight out of Logan. Presumptuous. How does she know so much about me, how I drive, how I pack, if I've had breakfast yet?

"What about the weather?" I ask, hopefully. I'm still terrified of flying, certain that any plane I board is destined to make tomorrow's headlines. Until two years ago, I'd never flown at all, an eccentric who could say, "I don't fly," as my father's mother long ago would pick up the telephone and say, "Operator, I don't dial." I embellished my defiant "I've never flown" with sickening effusions about trains and ships, and clichés about loving the journey as much as the arrival, about wanting to experience the dignity of distances and landscapes by allowing them their proper portion of time. When you look out the window of a plane from New York to Florida it takes two hours and forty minutes and all you saw, except at either end, is blue and white, air and clouds. But by train entire states ground endlessly by and you see fields and cows and villages and slums and folks sitting on the porch.

Not lies, exactly, but elaborate evasions. When it occurred to me that my grandmother didn't dial because she was illiterate, I began to suspect that my flying phobia was also a form of illiteracy, and I forced myself onto a plane. And then another, and another, thinking always of Carole Lombard, Glenn Miller, Leslie Howard. By some miracle, so far I've survived.

I'm at the airport less than two hours later, in plenty of time, just as the clerk promised. Strapped into a window seat (I always try for a window seat, eager not to be taken by surprise), I feel my heartbeat accelerate along with the plane as it zooms up the runway, flapping its arms for the takeoff, a race between heart and plane as to which will fail first. I try to think of my father, but I can't. Instead, I take deep breaths, observing through the window every detail, feeling the wonder of it, knowing that it can't be done, that it's all illusion, a trick accomplished by a suspension of disbelief, for proof of which I have only to look at the vapid, calm-polished faces of the flight-attendants and hear the bored mid-western drawl of Captain Marvel, the pilot.

The plane lifts off, noses up, is smoothly, almost perpendicularly airborne, while I hold my breath, waiting for it to smash into something, to blow apart, to stumble, to lurch, to plummet. In spite of me, it rises with bland self-assurance while Boston recedes below, transmogrified into a neat, complicated board game, made less and less real by distance until it's a toy and then nothing, and we are in sunshine with a bed of fleece beneath us, looking as soft and safe as a feather mattress. Still, when the flight-attendants at last come around pushing the beverage cart, I buy two Bloody Marys and drink them too quickly so that, even after I've consumed the snack, I feel stupefied.

I think of my dream of Angie. If I were back in analysis, I'd spend hours on that dream, beginning with a memory of standing in the doorway of the house we rented that last long summer two years ago in the Rockies. I am standing high above the lake, looking down at Angie as she rows away from shore, a floppy green cotton sun-hat pulled down over her ears, rowing out in the little boat to fish, as she did nearly every day. I watch until she and the boat are a speck way out in the middle of the lake, little more than punctuation, feeling an urgent impulse to call her back, to make certain she is real. And then I am crying because part of me can't help wishing Angie would turn out to be nothing but a dot on the horizon, after all. I am feeling bruised by the hopelessness. Still, though Angie has been gone only quarter of an hour, I miss her achingly. It's terrible to know that my heart will be no more broken without Angie than it is with her.

I must have fallen asleep because the next thing I know, the plane is about to land, and it's time for more fear. I grip the armrests and watch this bluer sea and greener earth rise and, in the rising, lose their geometry. The plane touches down. *Touches* down! A euphemism, an outrageous understatement for the dreadful rushing grinding gasping shuddering perilous irresponsible caracole gambado buck-jump of a return from airborne to earthbound. Still, once again I've survived.

When the carousel yields up my suitcase, I step out-side into the flat glare of the Florida sunshine, sniff the unseasonable air, feel the heat. Perhaps I've died, after all, and those were the gates of hell that automatically slid open to let me through, a hell with palm trees and taxis, one of which I manage to snare. I've been up and down, there and here, north and south, shivering and hot, afraid only for myself, barely thinking of my father who may already have died, and now I'm being swept along in this air-conditioned cab that winds out of Ft. Lauderdale, crosses a bridge, then proceeds down Ocean Drive where the high-rises begin, the huge whipped-cream condos somewhere beyond whose ranks, cleverly concealed, lies an ocean.

Florida depresses me. Florida is a morning when my father and I come down to the lobby in one of the bank of high-speed elevators, to be greeted as we exit by a knot of aged men in Bermuda shorts, knee socks, and short-sleeved shirts with paisley ascots at their necks, lounging about like drug store cowboys. At the sight of my father, their faces flicker with life. "Whaddya say, Max," one of them calls out. "Wanna go to the bank and cash a check?"

Later, I wrote a poem about the terrible emptiness of their sun-drowned golden days between power (goodbye, my teeth) and death. "So many deaths," my father said, soon after he and my mother moved to Florida. "Someone's always dying. But what can you expect? That's what they come down here for."

Is it his turn now? In spite of his longstanding hypo-chondria, it's difficult for me to imagine him broken in health. In one way or another, directly, indirectly, in obei-sance to or, more often, in revolt against, so much of my life (I'm ashamed even to admit it to myself) has been dominated by him, that ignorant, shrewd, unfeeling, selfish, sentimental, graceless, unsubtle, self-pitying, despotic, embarrassing, aggressive, angry, unkind, charming, disapproving, violent, energetic, humorless rock who never gave me a word I could take away with me to a dark corner of my life, no wisdom, no comfort, no love, just the cold hard glare of negative judgment, of arithmetic, of the practical arrangements of survival as he conceived them in his singleminded clawup from less-than-nothing despised lower-east-side-kike to what seemed to him eminence: the Cadillac traded in every two years, the Norman castle overlooking the Hudson River with its dozens of rooms and acres and its Olympic-sized swimming pool in which, for a few years, even he swam, gasping and thrashing like some archaic sea monster out of its depth.

The taxi pulls off the street into a semi-circular drive, stopping beneath a broad green and white striped canopy, where I send it on its way. A tanned Cuban youth in a crisp white shirt takes my suitcase. I follow him through the garden-green lobby with its trellised walls whose wallpaper simulates climbing vines, and into a merry tune-filled elevator in whose mirrored rear I confront myself, startled as always by the disparity between my mind's eye self and this other literal one. I am larger and older than I can ever remember, and only half as good-looking. It's no use trying to adapt to the changing physical facts; I am always, probably mercifully, years behind. I am half a century old and menopausal, but inside little has been settled. Inside I'm an intricate, slovenly network of crossed purposes, forever waiting to be surprised into joy, ready for anything. All the rest is temporary; my exile and loneliness are merely a pause for breath. I turn my back on the matron in the mirror, reverting to my true self (thin, eighteen, reckless) and watch the shifting red numbers above the door as they count, predictably, 11, 12, 14, deceiving the 14th floor tenants into luck.

Arrived at the ultimate floor, which calls itself PH for penthouse, the youth and I walk to the extreme end of a long blue-carpeted corridor where I exchange a dollar for my suitcase. I ring the bell. After a time, just as I've begun to think that my mother, who isn't expecting me until tomorrow, is out, probably at the hospital or the mortuary, I hear the sliding, ratcheting, complicated, deep metal sounds of a number of locks being sprung. The door opens, framing my mother.

"You!" she cries, her face echoing the voiced shout, a mixture of surprise and delight. "I was just sitting here waiting for your call. You said tomorrow." She throws her arms around me and begins to cry.

TWO (now)

The intensive care room surprises me; it's so huge and noisy, as busy and unprivate as a bus terminal. Who would dare to die in such a lively place? How could you die in a place where you can't even sleep?

Although my father is being intensely cared for, he looks the same to me. He looks strong and his color is good. He smiles weakly when he sees me. Bravely.

"So soon?" he says as I lean to kiss him. "Mother said tomorrow."

"Progress," I say. "If men can get from Florida to the moon, I guess I can make it from New Hampshire to Florida."

"*Progress!*" my father says. "Look what's keeping me alive." He lowers the sheet to reveal a small box taped to his chest. Behind him, on the wall, his heartbeat dances on a television screen. The beat is even, regular. Thank God he can't see it. It would kill me to watch my own heartbeat. "The doctor says if it wasn't for this gadget I'd have been a goner."

"Shah!" my mother, who never speaks Yiddish, says. "Don't even mention it."

"Facts are facts."

"It's working okay?"

"Tomorrow it goes inside."

"The first one wasn't working right," my mother says "They weren't sure if it was the machine or the heart. But this one, knock wood."

A plump young nurse approaches with a thermometer. "Hello, gorgeous," my father says. "How about tonight, after work?"

"In front of your wife?" the nurse says, putting the thermometer in his mouth and grabbing his pulse.

"Don't mind me," my mother says cheerfully.

"All the vital signs look promising," I say, and my father does a Groucho Marx bit with his eyebrows.

"He's much better than I expected," I tell my mother a little later, driving back from the hospital. "He was always such a coward."

"Can you believe it?"

"Remember when he had that cold and insisted on having nurses around the clock?"

My mother laughs. "It was more than a cold. It was flu. And it was only a little while after Grandpa died of pneumonia."

I guide the mammoth Cadillac on its cushion of air through the traffic. It's like driving a small hotel. Driving a hotel past hotels.

"He's so relieved to be alive," my mother says. "Thank you-know-Who."

The increasing sound of a siren accumulates behind us, and I pull over. The siren overtakes and passes us, diminishing ahead. I once wrote a poem with the Doppler effect as metaphor. It was a poem about Angie, going away.

"The rescue squad," my mother says. "That's what I called for Daddy. I swear they were there in less than two minutes."

What a comfort, I think, and how human. In New York, a man I knew spent the first ten hours of his death on a sidewalk with people carefully walking around him, assuming he was drunk.

"They die anyhow," my mother says.

"I don't know how you can live in a place where death is practically all that happens?"

"It happens later here. How many women my age do you know in New York play golf three times a week?"

"Dad is always saying he'd have been dead long ago if he hadn't been living here. But I don't know if it's worth it if that's all he thinks about."

"You don't know the half of it. Every minute he keeps me abreast of the current events of his body. Bowels, circulation, this pain, that pain, dizziness, gas, nausea." She sighs. "I tell him relax, things can only get worse, be glad you're alive even if it hurts."

But I know he's the kind of man who will hang on as long as there's an ounce of strength to complain with. Not my mother. She is seventy-five, only a few years younger, but more than once she's told me, "If I have a stroke, if my mind ever begins to go, if I ever get so that I can't play golf, no support systems, understand?"

"Every day is a gift," she says. "I really believe that."

It's true; she rarely complains, is genuinely surprised at her luck. She thought she was going to die young, and she's already more than twenty years older than her own father.

"But I miss them," she says, sighing. "Four already this year. Ray, Nat, Sylvia, Rose. Flora says they're dying like hotcakes." We both laugh. Flora is my mother's closest

- 12 -

friend and her malapropisms have brightened our lives for years.

"How is Flora?" I ask.

"Except for her post-natal drip, she's in A-mint condition."

THREE (now)

My mother and I are having our first preprandial drink in what they call the den, though it's no snug and private retreat, merely an area of a vast green ambience that also includes the formal living area, rarely used, a card nook, and the dining area, all more or less open to each other and arranged upon a meadow, a grassy lea of sculptured green carpet that yawns from wall to distant wall where windows frame *trompe l'oeil* views of sea and sky in colors so improbable that they can only be real. As Angie said, there's a lot of bad art in nature.

But there is more bad art in art, examples of which hang on these walls, chosen by my father whose eye for style fails him beyond the boundaries of the garment district where he so successfully labored for much of his life. There are three paintings of tropical beaches, purchased on a trip to some Caribbean paradise, white sailboats on the horizon painted in day-glo colors. The dominant painting is of a bowl of wax fruit, a still-lifeless, Angie called it, or *nature double-morte*. It reminds me of the apartment Angie and I shared, the one I fled for New Hampshire, whose ugly little lobby was decorated with a fake fountain ringed with artificial flowers, changed seasonally by the superintendent, daffodils and tulips in spring, roses in summer, mums and dahlias in autumn. In the winter it's bare, except at Christmas when a frosted white plastic tree appears with blinking electric candles. Art and artifice. Angie loved it. The one brief time she was down here with me she loved these paintings, too, remarking that what was so exciting was that the perpetrators were sincere, as my father was, or so she assumed, and that like books, whether they're literature or entertainment, they all say something about the society we live in. The difference is in the long run. Like the fake flowers, entertainment needs constant renewal.

"But what about these pictures?" I asked. "My parents are permanently satisfied with them."

"They hung them and never saw them again," Angie said, "and, besides, the long run takes longer."

Angie's studio is three flights up in an old warehouse off Hudson Street. It's what she calls The Serious Place, and, unlike anywhere or anything else of hers, it's surprisingly neat and well organized. There she's in complete control. She knows where everything is and every space has its reason. A good carpenter, she built handsome off-the-floor cupboards and stalls for her finished work, and shelves for her supplies, and movable wall-sized panels where she hangs the more recent paintings, those she's working on and the finished ones she still needs to have around her. A toilet and sink stand unenclosed in a corner, and next to the sink a small table with a hotplate, and on the hotplate a red enamel saucepan, and off in another corner a cot with a blanket and three pillows, and these, and the separate receptacle for emptied wine bottles, are her only concession to her non-painting self.

It's a large square room with good light, but the light can hardly matter since when she is what she calls "inside the painting," she sometimes paints all night, and if the electricity were to go off, she would paint by candlelight. One blizzardy February morning, because she hadn't come home all night, I stopped by to make sure she was all right and to bring her some breakfast. She was completely absorbed in the painting she was doing, that she'd been doing all night, despite the fact that the heat had failed. She wore layers of sweaters under her coat and her fur-lined snow boots, a knitted hat pulled far down over her ears and a muffler wound around her neck. Only her hands were bare and they were two shades of blue, one from the cold. She looked as if she could barely keep hold of the brush, but the face she turned toward me when she was aware of my presence, was haggard and feverish with excitement. And what a painting it was!

"I can't stop now," she said in a faint, breathless voice, dismissing me.

Later, during our summer in the Montana Rockies, I saw that Angie's colors were all out of those landscapes of her childhood, though the landscapes themselves, the mountains, trees, lake, snow, aren't recognizably there. The paintings are lyrical and mysterious, almost mystical, but they have the depth and movement of those landscapes with their winds and waters, weathers and seasons.

Angie, Angie. She was christened Evelyn-Angelica, with the hyphen. Only her mother ever called her by that given name, and never with love. She was a strict, rigid woman of German stock, hardworking, demanding, unimaginative, and severe. "Every Monday the furniture was polished," Angie told me. "Every Tuesday dinner of my early life was split pea soup. Every day of the week was like that, with its appointed chores and unchanging menu. I can't hear the word Thursday without smelling its smells and hearing its sounds. Thursday smells of cabbage and ham hocks and sounds of carpets on a line being whacked with a carpet beater."

"What's a carpet beater? What are ham hocks?" I asked, loving her. "God, Angie, you're so exotic!"

"And all around us the most improbably beautiful scenery in the world." I hadn't seen it yet. "The towering snow-capped mountains, the great, tall, looming firs, the vast cherry orchards sloping down to the shores of the huge lake with its changing colors, its moody surface; the wild sunsets, the endless sky." Her father, an engineer, was on his way to a job in California when the scenery stopped him in his tracks. He took a job with the national parks service as a forest ranger, never making it to the coast. Her mother was a schoolteacher. The teachers were shamefully underpaid. "We're paid one third in dollars, two thirds in scenery," they said. "Though I doubt my mother ever said that; she was humorless. Anyhow, the contrast between that wild and powerful landscape and our rigid narrow domestic life was impossible to reconcile. It's why I'm incapable of doing anything I'm supposed to do, or in the way I'm expected to do it. I hate schedules, routines. I can't have my meals according to the clock, or go to bed because it's supposed to be bedtime, or get up because somewhere a cock is crowing."

I had just finished setting the table. There were candles and fall flowers and I stood back to admire the festive look of it. It was seven-thirty. Acting on a compelling familial urge left over from my recent past, I'd spent the last four hours making a turkey dinner with, as they say, all the trimmings. It was our first Thanksgiving together, my first ever without blood relatives of any kind. Jed was with Herbie for the long weekend, Nick was in school way out west, too far to come home. I wasn't exactly lonely, but I did want a semblance of something like roots, tradition, a small pocket of warmth and ceremony in the improvisational schemelessness of our time together. But Angie wasn't having it. She was sipping burgundy and reminiscing and the apartment was full of rich, delicious smells that were making me mad with nostalgia and hunger.

But the turkey was drying out in the oven. The marshmallows had long since melted into the sweet potato casserole, and the gravy had a skin on it. My beautiful dinner. "Damn it," I said, "it's Thanksgiving, the only holiday I like. Think how hard I've been working to provide some semblance of normal home life."

"There's no such thing."

". . . a lovely, traditional occasion. Just this once, if I promise never to do it again, couldn't you make an exception?"

What I hadn't yet learned was that, like most alcoholics, Angie wasn't hungry.

"The magic, the mystery," she said, lifting her hands, opening them out like a Balinese dancer, as if shaping the contours of a vase of exquisite, ghostly blooms. She talked a lot about magic and mystery, two things of which I was the murderer. Angie put down her glass and came and stood on my feet. She was smaller than I and didn't weigh much, and she was barefoot and she liked to stand on my feet, her arms around my neck.

"I'm standing on your feet," she said.

"I know."

"You can't be mad at someone when they're standing on your feet."

I laughed. Angie laughed. We began to dance that way, with Angie standing on my feet. Earlier, we had made love and we still smelled faintly of each other. I was over-come with love. And I was hungry.

"Okay," I said. "I'll do this feast solo. You can pick at it whenever."

"No, my darling, my love," she said, opening a new bottle of wine and filling our glasses, "Sit down. We'll do this one together. You cooked. I'll serve."

My eyes, following thought, move from that other in-terior time to absorb the details of this present, so very dif-ferent one. The cluster of furniture in the den area includes a reclining (heart-ease) chair where my mother is sitting; my father's desk on which mail, much of it from the financial sector of New York City where most of his money is conser-vatively invested, is piling up; a convertible sofa, uncom-fortable in both its functions, on which I am sitting; an en-tertainment center which includes a mammoth French pro-vincial bleached fruitwood console that houses a 26-inch color TV set and an AM/FM stereo radio and phonograph, the latter rarely used. The television console, its huge eye staring blindly, is flanked by two narrow bookcases. Among the detritus on their shelves, some of my life's work is in-cluded, two slender volumes, a few chapbooks, a couple of anthologies containing several of my poems and short sto-ries, and a handful of literary quarterlies in which I am also modestly represented.

Not much. I was a late bloomer.

"You've become an early drinker," I tell my mother, because it's barely half past four and because Angie is still present. Ah, the cocktail hour, I'd say, watching Angie pour her first drink of the new day, not long after opening her bleared, bloodshot eyes to it. This drink was restorative, would clear and brighten her gaze, briefly transform her into that fey and funny, lighter-than-air creature I adored. But there would be more drinks. Gradually, she would slide into the pouting, mumbling child, and soon the angry child, the still angrier child, and then the monster spewing hate and venom, unbelievable hours of that with its wake of violence and destruction, with its incredibly bottomless energy that, thank God, finally gave way to the sodden exhausted vegetable collapsing into something deeper than sleep, only a little less than death. She was on what she so innocently called "a toot." My poor lost Angie. I genuinely grieved when I could allow disgust to give way to pity and despair. The toots were growing more and more frequent, and I had no idea why or what to do about them.

My mother explains that she only drinks before dinner. And dinner is so early, six o'clock.

"Well, then, why is dinner so early?" I ask. My mother is smoking, and I try not to think about it. Why do they shorten their days as they grow older and the days grow fewer? Does it have to do with energy and the fear that it will give out before they've performed the fewer and fewer acts the day will hold? I don't yet realize, as I will later, that time shortens itself. How the world narrows with all the compromises age exacts, and especially with the shrinking future that scarcely stretches beyond tomorrow, next week, next month. Energy and time. My poem, sitting up north in my typewriter, yellowing, waiting in my head. I look at my mother, wondering when that moment arrives, and if it arrives all at once, that moment when you lose the belief that there is still time for everything, when you know you may never finish Proust, never learn mushrooms. How does it feel, that first and most decisive death? My mother is admirable and brave, devoid of self-pity, uncomplaining, and absolutely unready to slip into decrepitude. I blur the focus of my gaze against the betraying skin and see that she still looks young and trim in outline if not in detail, gamely defying the years, hiding behind cosmetics that grow more ingenious as the need grows greater. Her strawberry blonde hair is teased into an elaborate arrangement and frozen there by some fixative that gives it a texture so far removed from the original that if someone tried to sell her a wig of the same material she'd be furious, horrified. I have a vision of her waking each morning to confront her image, seeing it more and more as the armature on which to sculpt the self she daily sends forth. Hers is a fierce and indomitable pride, the habit of vanity so common to beautiful women.

"How long are you planning to stay there, Annie?" she asks. "In New Hampshire?"

I watch the smoke slowly curling out of her mouth, her nose, feeling the longing inside my own mouth that may never leave me. How long? Measures of time. "You've been gone four cartons of cigarettes, even though I've been trying to quit," Angie wrote. "Please come home."

"I don't know," I say, honestly.

My mother sighs. "I only want you to be happy. I can see you're not happy."

"I'm not unhappy."

"Have you met anyone out there? In New Hampshire?"

"I wish you'd stop saying New Hampshire as though it's an emerging nation."

"You know what I mean."

What she means is have I met a man, the one I am going to marry next. I watch her light another cigarette, feeling in my own fingers, lips, mouth, the lovely lost gestures and sensations.

"You never give up," I say.

"No, why should I? I can't stand the thought of you living alone. It isn't natural."

She's right, of course. Living alone isn't natural. "I like living alone," I lie. "It's a luxury."

She snorts. "Some luxury!" We are silent for a while, thinking our own thoughts. Then she says, "There's someone here I want you to meet."

"Mother!"

"As soon as Daddy gets out of the hospital, I'm going to arrange it."

"I don't want to meet anyone."

"Why not? You know I won't die happy . . ."

"Nobody dies happy. Anyhow, you're a long way from dying."

"Does it hurt to meet someone? Don't you think you've been divorced long enough?"

I can't tell her that I don't think I can love a man again, that I've developed a sweet tooth. My mother smiles lovingly at me, not saying that I will always be her child, as she usually does, but gets up, instead, to go to the kitchen to freshen her drink. I follow, not reminding her that I was married for twenty years, gave her two grandchildren, raised them to manhood, have already gone that route. Ah, when I think of it! The mystery isn't what will become of me, how my life will change, but who that earlier person was. I feel so little connection, so little continuity. What remains of that other life? The children, of course, though they aren't children any more. The relics: books, photographs in albums, papers still in the vault. Memories. A few people. Yet it could as well have been someone else's life. I think, some-times, of that earlier self as if she were a daughter who died, except that I don't miss her. *I think of her in the third person.*

"Lots of women remarry at the first opportunity," my mother says. "There must be forty widows down here for every available man, and every one of them would give their eyeteeth, if they still had them."

I can only sigh.

"This one's very nice looking," my mother says. "And not that old."

"Not what old?"

"He's a real catch, Annie. His wife's family was Plaza Paper Products. You know, the PPP commercials? He's extremely wealthy."

"How long since she died, the PPP princess?"

"It must be at least a month."

"Mother!"

She laughs. "It's not as though it was sudden. It was a lingering death. She was sick for years."

FOUR: (Then)

    The aisle parted the wedding guests down the middle: his right, hers left. Ann proceeded down it on her father's arm, her thighs sliding in rhythm against the creamy satin folds of her gown, while a corner of her mind directed her feet not to tangle with its train. She was grateful for the veil that curtained her face, though it had seemed such an idiotic symbol in a ceremony filled with idiotic symbols, because it fuzzed the outlines of what was taking place (she couldn't have borne to see it clearly), and it also obscured the cornered animal lurking behind her eyes, the part of her that desperately wanted to bolt and run.

    They came without mishap to the end of their march, where Herbie and the rabbi waited. She was the last to arrive, the star, bursting like an orgasm onto the scene after the mounting tension of all the foreplay. "Ahhh, here comes the bride!"

    Her father handed her over to Herbie, gave her away to this gangling youth, this stranger she had known less than a year ago. The costliness of the occasion affirmed his satisfaction at giving her away. A reverse ransom; no price was too great to pay for the incredible luck of unloading her, a transaction that was the culmination of nearly twenty-two years of being the Jewish father of a female child. *Here: she's your burden now do with her what you will if she'll let you I don't know much more about you than meets the eye but what the hell I'm thankful to you for snatching her not a minute too soon from the jaws of spinsterhood or almost as bad from union with one of those pishers she was always falling in love with the radicals and intellectuals she was ready to starve in an attic with but you at least look a little more normal you don't talk crazy though God only knows.*

She took her place beside Herbie. Her father stepped back and the rabbi stepped forward. Surrounded by men. She may have been the star, the focus, but the ceremony, like the world, remained theirs. The rabbi was short, not much older than Herbie. None of them had ever laid eyes on him before yesterday's rehearsal. She wondered where her parents had found him, if there was an agency that placed freelance rabbis. If they were that secular, why did there have to be a rabbi at all, and why was her father wearing a hat, his prized Borsalino?

She slumped out of kindness, to make the rabbi feel less short, but when he began to speak and she saw that he was arrogant and stupid, a mechanical rabbi, she pulled herself back up to her full height and tried not to listen. The bower beneath which they stood was a cascade of spring flowers. There were flowers everywhere, wall to wall. There might not be enough oxygen to go around. Suffocating, she took deep noisy breaths with her mouth open, a fish drowning in honeyed air, while the rabbi paused to stare at her, his own mouth open on a suspended platitude. She closed her mouth and tried to breathe normally while the rabbi continued his eulogy. They were the future, young and courageous, and Herbie was a soldier in uniform fighting Hitler and fascism and, especially, anti-Semitism (he was in the public relations department at Wright Field in Dayton,

Ohio) and she, Ann, was going to stand by his side, be his helpmeet. Compliant, she soon heard herself agreeing to love, honor, and even obey this good brave youth for however long it took. In three months she would be twenty-two. In less than three years she would begin her nervous breakdown. It would take her twenty years to tell Herbie that she had changed her mind. In almost thirty years, she would be sitting in a Florida condominium listening to her mother talk to her as though she were a twenty-one year old spinster again.

Thank God the future was also veiled!

Through her peripheral vision, she watched Herbie to see how he was taking it. His face was properly serious, but not grim. Only a moment ago she had thought of him as a gangling youth, but he was sweet, graceful, fair and uncomplicated. He was uncommonly handsome. For the fiftieth time in twenty-four hours she assured herself that she loved him, a quiet, undramatic, comfortable kind of love, and that of course she was doing the right thing. Life with Jake would have been impossible. Pang. Don't think of Jake.

The service limped on, the rabbi contriving to sound as if he had known them all their lives, Herbie, Ann, their proud, happy parents. Fortunately, his imagination was as limited as his intelligence and in time he was emptied. His sidekick, a cantor, broke into a plaintive tune. Poor Jews, Ann thought, what do we know from joy? Even our humor is soggy with sorrow. She turned a dial in her head and heard the mighty strains of Death and Transfiguration, also inappropriate, but very loud. She sipped the sweet heavy wine of the blessing. Herbie took her moist hand in his cool dry one and slid the ring, symbol of entrapment, not around her neck but onto her finger, and then he was vigorously stamping his heel on the napkin-wrapped glass, smashing it, scattering demons, mourning Jerusalem, and the assembled guests broke their silence in a murmuring rush of approval. She and Herbie turned to each other. He lifted her veil and leaned to kiss her in their first sanctioned embrace while flashbulbs popped. "Mine, all mine," he whispered, leering, and she laughed, relieved, exhausted, trapped, and then they were swept off to be kissed and feted in an ante-chamber where champagne corks exploded and a nuptial board groaned beneath smoked fish oozing oils, myriad-eyed caviar twinkling beneath chandeliers, the livers of a hundred chickens sautéed in their own fat, chopped and sculpted into the shape of a brooding hen surrounded by a year of her eggs, deviled. There were platters and platters of canapés and knishes and blanketed cocktail franks, all of it merely prelude to the formal feast that awaited in yet another of the hotel's salons.

Not much later, Ann would see her first photographs of concentration camp victims and she would recall with horror that this wedding was going on at the very same time!

They were engulfed by embracing women, Herbie still holding onto her hand, the mothers and sisters and aunts and grandmothers. Ann's mother was crazy about Herbie. Even her father, who had vehemently disliked Al, barely tolerated Morty, and ridiculed Jake, had more than once said of Herbie, (though everything he said he said more than once) "You can't help liking him." It was true.

"My baby," her mother said, putting a glass of champagne in Ann's hand and toasting her with her own. "My own little *ketzelah*." Ann was half a head taller than her mother. There were tears in her mother's eyes, but she was smiling with happiness. Ann would miss her; she had expected that. But she now saw that her mother would miss her, too. Recently, she and her mother had become friends. She grinned at her mother and said, "You're not losing a daughter, you're gaining a Herbie."

"So how does it feel to be Mrs. Herbert Alan Becker?" Aunt Millie asked, beaming.

The question startled her. She wanted to run to a mirror to see if she looked any different. Because, yes, that was who she was now. Immutably altered, for better or worse. She turned again to look at Herbie, trying to read in the man she already knew, his becoming, and possibly her own. The crowd of surrounding women had been joined by men who were slipping folded checks into Herbie's breast pockets, or pressing envelopes containing war bonds into his hands. Here's your reward, kiddo. He saw Ann looking at him and gave a small, private version of his charming crooked grin. She was reassured. Anyone who could smile like that couldn't be all bad. Jake would not have smiled. He would have guessed what she was feeling and looked at her with eyes that were understanding, gentle. But, then, he never would have been a party to this kind of wedding. She reached for Herbie's hand, the one free of war bonds, and squeezed it.

They made toasts and jokes and ate and drank and smoked and danced and sang and laughed and cut the cake and cried and had pictures taken so that every moment of this event, the marrying of Ann Silver and Herbert Alan Becker, would be recorded, frozen in the posed and candid attitudes struck by the actual participants. Whatever changes the years wrought, these photographs would remain to certify that this had truly happened in this particular way on this particular day.

"I've had it with this party," Herbie said. They were on the dance floor, both more than a little drunk. "We've eaten everything in sight, the place is a shambles, and I've done my duty and danced with every woman in the house. Let's get out of here."

"Okay. Let's go somewhere and consummate our union. Consummate means to perfect. Did you know that?"

"Perfection is what I'm after." He rattled the key in his pocket, the key to the bridal suite on the 27th floor of this same hotel. She looked around the room at the revelers, their chairs pushed back from the wrecked tables, their eyes heavy, blue cigar smoke curling up to form stagnant clouds that hung beneath the chandeliers. No one was paying the slightest attention to them. They slipped away.

They rode up in the elevator with a stocky pink-faced navy lieutenant and a woman with teased gold hair and a bright red mouth.

"Oh how quaint," the woman said. "A bride. And this handsome sergeant is the groom, am I right?"

"Right, beautiful," Herbie said, grinning. "We've escaped from the wedding party and are at this very moment ascending to the nuptial chamber." He smiled lovingly at Ann. "She's a slut but she's managed to hang onto one last shred of her virginity. We're going to change all that and make an honest woman of her."

"God, Herbie, you're drunk," Ann said. "Don't feel you have to blabber everything to all our new friends."

"How come you never marry me?" the woman whined to the lieutenant.

"We only just met three hours ago."

"God, it seems so much longer."

"And I bet you're no virgin, are you, Carole-Margaret."

"I used to be, but I didn't like it."

"I haven't been too crazy about it, myself," Ann said, admiringly.

"So what stopped you?"

"Stupidity. My upbringing. Nice girls don't." It was true. She knew of only one of her friends who had gone all the way and she was thought of as cheap.

"How'd you know you were a nice girl?"

The operator stopped the elevator at the nineteenth floor and slid the door open.

"Why don't you come up to our room so we can continue this conversation?" Ann asked, hopefully. She liked Carole-Margaret. The subject interested her.

"You two have more important things to do," the lieutenant said, winking at Herbie.

"What about us?" Carole-Margaret said. "What we have to do isn't important? Is that what you're saying?"

"Sweetheart, I'm not saying anything of the sort."

"What are you saying

"Nothing. I'm not saying . . ."

"Just because I'm a cheap bimbo pickup you think I have no feelings? You think this isn't important to me?" She leaned into a corner of the elevator and began to sob. The elevator operator, a stooped old man, half-turned, smirking impatiently. "I'm just another lay in just another port, right?"

"Come on, now, sweetheart, you're holding up this elevator."

"I don't care if I'm holding up the entire second world war, sailor, what do you think of that?"

"I think that's dandy, Carole-Margaret. Now let's go."

"Give me a handkerchief. My nose is running."

"You can blow your nose when we get to the room, sweetheart," the lieutenant said through clenched teeth. "There'll be Kleenex in the room. Now come on out of here."

"I don't wanna blow my nose in any fuckin' Kleenex and I'm not going anywhere with a cheap bastard who can't offer me his fuckin' handkerchief."

Herbie took a handkerchief from his pocket, shook out the folds, and held it to her nose.

"Here, Carole-Margaret, blow your nose in my fuckin' handkerchief," he said sweetly.

The elevator operator did a little shuffle and looked imploringly at them while the woman, smiling through her tears at Herbie, blew her nose. The door closed and the elevator ascended.

"Might as well ride up while you're blowing your nose," the elevator man said. "I'll drop you off on the way down."

"How come every time I meet the man of my dreams," Carole-Margaret wailed, looking with love at Herbie, "he's married?"

"We can still have it annulled," Ann offered.

'My apologies to both of you," the lieutenant said. "What a way to start a marriage."

"It's been fun," Ann said.

At their floor, Carole-Margaret kissed Herbie good-bye ("forever," she sobbed) on the mouth, and Herbie and the lieutenant smartly saluted each other. "I'm going home," they heard Carole-Margaret say as the door slid closed behind them. "I wouldn't fuck you for all the rice in China."

"What a gift for friendship you have," Ann said to Herbie as he carried her across the threshold of the bridal suite. "Yech, more flowers!"

Coming out of the elegant bathroom a little later, elaborately prepared, wearing one of the trousseau gowns provided by her mother who knew how to marry off a daughter, Ann said, "So how *did* I know I was a nice girl? Why did I believe all that garbage?"

"I hope you're not going to worry about that now," Herbie said. He was already in the huge bed awaiting her in brand new navy blue silk pajamas with white piping. "You look gorgeous."

"So do you."

"We're both so dressed up for the occasion," he laughed. "And the first order of business is to tear off this costly finery."

"You're so romantic, Herbie."

"Everything I know I learned at the movies."

She curled her arms around his neck. "You know, you're actually pretty cute. Okay, let's begin."

He laughed, and then she did, too. They were so comfortable together.

"Let's hope that after all the sofas and automobile seats," he said, "I'll know how to make love in an actual bed."

"I just hope that after all the necking and petting I'll like actual intercourse."

'It gets to be habit-forming, so it must be good."

They had been making love almost from the day they'd met and, although she hungered to feel him inside her, she always came anyway, as he did. She believed that orgasms were the inevitable outcome of sexual arousal, the prize you were really going for, much as you enjoyed the crackerjacks along the way. But now, ready though she was, when he tried to enter her she cried out in pain and he withdrew.

"Is it done?" she asked as though it were a surgical procedure, as it was.

"No."

"Do it."

Later, with Herbie asleep beside her, she wondered why mindless nature had given women this obdurate barrier and given men nothing corresponding to it. She felt outraged. And still angrier because a man had given a male name, the name of the god of marriage, to her maidenhead, a god guardian. Angry, she fell asleep.

When she opened her eyes again, Herbie was leaning on an elbow, watching her. He smiled. "Good morning. Have you got a hangover?"

"It can't be morning," she mumbled, trying to remember where she was and why.

"It's past ten. You want to make love again?"

"Hell no."

"Then I'll call down for breakfast. What do you feel like?"

"Everything."

He ordered orange juice, scrambled eggs, French toast, blueberry pancakes, bacon, ham, sausages, croissants, pots of coffee. When it arrived, he signed the check with a flourish, a worldly man who had been signing checks all his life, whose signature was a promise as good as cash. He would go on doing this all his life, never worried about whether there would be anything to back up his promises. John Hancock *sans peur*, she would dub him.

This bill, however, would be paid by Ann's father. But once they left the hotel the wedding was over and they would be on their own. They were on their honeymoon. The honeymoon was the drive to Dayton, Ohio where, in three days, Herbie would resume his duties at Wright Field, helping Major Donnelly issue press releases and entertain visiting dignitaries. Before the end of his freshman year, Herbie had been plucked by his country from the Wharton School of Business. It took him eight months to charm his way out of the tail of a bomber that made anti-submarine runs over the North Atlantic. There was little or no combat, but even so it was a dangerous place to be; you never knew when, out of boredom, which was rampant, the pilot would become frisky, as he often did and, as it happened, did once too often on an afternoon foray when, following a routine morning run in which he had participated, Herbie was sent to the infirmary with what turned out to be flu. The Lucky Flu, he thereafter called it, for by dusk of that day the eight men in his crew, and a ninth, his replacement, were stupidly and unnecessarily dead and partly cremated. All his life thereafter, Herbie would be aware of the thin thread by which his life hung, but instead of this making him more reverent of that life, as it should have done, it made him careless. Whether this was because he believed himself to be charmed or because, knowing the chanciness of fate he couldn't be bothered with the rules, Ann was never sure.

He had no idea what he would do if the war ever ended. The war was so omnipresent, had been going on for so long, that it was impossible for either of them to see beyond it. The future would have to take care of itself.

"So this is marriage," Ann said when they were in the car, her father's wedding present to them, a small black Pontiac, not too used, one of the last off the assembly lines before the war curtailed production. It was undistinguished, but they were overjoyed to have it.

"Don't you like marriage?" Herbie asked. They were emerging from the tunnel into New Jersey.

"Ours isn't real," she said. "I only did it to shut my parents up. Also, to get away from them."

"Thanks a lot."

"What did you do it for?"

"For this car, honey. My first car. See how nicely it works."

"Marriage was supposed to be what came next."

"Only 36,000 miles on it, practically new. Good rubber. Doesn't seem to be shooting oil."

"Go, couple off with someone, Annie, and drive off together into the setting sun. I tried to get out of it the night before the wedding but my mother wouldn't let me. 'All these people are coming.' she pointed out. 'And what about the caterers?'"

"How nicely it handles. Watch. I turn the steering wheel a little to the right and the car goes that way. This wheel in my hands must be connected in some way to those big rubber wheels out there."

She looked mournfully out at New Jersey. "Look at all that garbage."

"That's not garbage, it's industry. This great nation. What we're fighting for."

"It smells," she said, closing the window. He reached to turn on the radio. The Andrews Sisters.

". . . with anyone else but me, anyone else but me," Herbie sang along. "My God, even the radio works. Your father's a champion."

His hands were firm and steady on the wheel, good hands, square, clean, capable, handsomely made like the rest of him. She had read somewhere, perhaps everywhere, that you could tell a lot about people from their hands.

"I like your hands," she said.

"You'll learn to like other parts of me as well," he said. "You'll see."

"I already do." They drove on without talking, through a Lucky Strike commercial. She turned the radio off and said, "That rabbi made me want to vomit. Jesus, Herbie, change the landscape, can't you?"

"In a minute."

"Didn't he make you want to vomit?"

"No, I liked the little fellow. He was spunky. He had to get up in front of all those people he'd never seen before and do his job."

"A rabbi, Herbie. A spiritual leader."

"Don't you think he was sincere?"

"Jesus, Herbie, how could he have been sincere?"

"Earnest, then. He was definitely earnest. He had to say something."

"I wish he had just done the ceremony and skipped all that nonsense."

"It was a big expensive audience." He turned the radio back on. "He felt more was required. Woody Herman."

"He was supposed to be sanctifying our union, not showing off for an audience."

"My, you're in a foul mood," he said fondly. "If that's what losing your virginity does to you I'm glad it's a

- 36 -

one-time event." He was silent for a moment. "Do you realize that we're having our first quarrel?"

"We've had hundreds."

"Our first married quarrel. The first of many, I
hope."

FIVE (Then)

The radio played all across Pennsylvania and most of Ohio. "Woody Herman," Herbie would say, and "Woody Herman Melville," Ann would reply, playing a game she had invented for the occasion called "Literary Snob." Among others, there had been Harry Henry James, Artie George Bernard Shaw, Glenn Henry Miller, Tommy Hardy Dorsey, and Benny Jonson Goodman.

"Kaye Kaiser and his Kollege of Musical Knowledge," Herbie said. "Oops, sorry. That's Shep Fields and his Rippling Rhythm."

She switched off the radio and turned to glare at him. She had been driving for the last two hours. "Talk to me," she said.

"I'm not supposed to be talking," he said. "I'm supposed to be resting."

"Couldn't we have a small restful conversation? Maybe even a serious one."

"After all these hours of marriage, what's left to say? Everything between us is settled."

"I bet you really mean that."

"We're nearly there," he said, yawning. "I hope you're going to like the apartment. If you were counting hen's teeth, you could say they were nearly as scarce as apartments in Dayton, Ohio. Wouldn't you think that with millions of Americans living in jungles, in mud, in trenches, in deserts, on beaches, in fields, in quonset huts, there'd be loads of apartments."

But Herbie had found them half of one. A week before leaving for New York for the wedding, he'd been standing in a cafeteria line behind two young women.

"Dodie's been transferred to Washington," he overheard one of them say. "What a luxury to have the whole place to myself."

"Can you afford it?" the other woman asked.

"Not really."

"Let me buy you lunch," Herbie said, and introduced himself. "I insist."

What a man!

"Never mind the apartment," Ann said. "I hope I'll like what's-her-name."

"Marbella."

"I can't imagine sharing an apartment with a total stranger named Marbella!"

"War is hell."

"So this is the lucky bride," was Marbella's dubious greeting as Ann and Herbie, knee deep in luggage, stood at the door. She was half a dozen years older than Ann, square jawed, strong boned, and handsome, with dark eyes that glittered at Ann like mica-shot stones, but melted when she turned to Herbie.

It was a pleasant, ordinary two bedroom, two bath apartment. Marbella had generously prepared the master bedroom for them. When they were at last safely inside it, with the door closed, Ann said, "This is some marriage. That woman is in love with you."

"Naturally. What did you expect?" He grinned happily, and started to unpack. "You take the top drawers, I'll take the bottom. I only need one, really."

Herbie and Marbella were breadwinners who went out into the world every day, so Ann took over the housekeeping. She had never had domestic responsibilities, except at summer camp where she had learned to make a bed with hospital corners and to sweep a floor, and the only cooking she had done was over a campfire or in grade school, where she had been taught to light an oven without blowing up the kitchen, and to make toast, oatmeal, and applesauce. Now, armed with *The Joy of Cooking*, she was prepared to scale new heights.

Between chores, she was writing a novel. She had been writing stories and poems from the age of eight, but she hadn't attempted a novel since the one she had begun when she was nine. It was called The Endless Novel because she had planned to go on writing it until she died, but she had given up on it when she was twelve. Later, rereading it, she could trace exactly what she had been reading at the time; each chapter mirrored its separate influence. She had begun with a Carolyn Keene heroine called Peggy, who had seemed incredibly witty to the eight-year-old Ann. By chapter three, Peggy was breeding collies, one of whom was killed on the road by a heedless driver speeding by at forty miles an hour. Two chapters later a hero appeared, a lean chap with steel-gray eyes and a strawberry roan. Not much later, Peggy was given a family, sisters and brothers, and there was a poignant scene in which the dearest of these died, while Ann wept into her copybook, smudging the ink. Then Peggy, whose name Ann now went back to the beginning to change to Katherine, was orphaned, stripped of friends and family, and cast bereft

- 40 -

and poverty-stricken into the cold and filthy London streets, and in short order, thanks to Zola and a large dose of Upton Sinclair, she began to give herself to larger, more selfless works. Although two of her fingers had fallen off in the freezing streets, she attempted to organize the workers in a glove factory, was thrown into jail and there stricken with consumption. Galsworthy appeared next, with Ann's struggle to get Katherine out of prison and into a drawing room, her deformed hand discreetly sheathed in the white gloves she wore while pouring tea and making witty remarks between coughing spells. Exhausted by so many transitions, she had put away The Endless Novel, promising herself that one day when her mind was more settled and her tastes less eclectic, she would return to it.

The novel she now embarked on would take place in a concentration camp. It would be a love story. The truth, the full horror of the camps was not yet known, but what they had learned was already incomprehensible enough to obsess Ann. Her hero was a frail, undersized fifteen-year-old Jewish musical prodigy, and the girl a nineteen-year-old athletic German Youth Corps fraulein, assigned to guard the Jewish children. The book would be about what it meant to have human feelings in a bestial world, to be innocent in the midst of such evil.

She grew more and more immersed in the book. She became both her characters, at one moment Noldi with his youthful yearnings, his terrors, his despair. Then she forced herself to be Elsa with her ramrod back and ripe young breasts, slowly beginning to question her rigid doctrinaire beliefs, among them that the inferior blood of Jews must not be allowed to pollute and weaken the blood of real Germans, that Hitler was the Messiah and could do no wrong. Ann crawled inside Elsa and breathed with her. Secretly, she brought her dead older brother's violin to Noldi. Watching his love of the music suffuse his pale, sensitive face while he played, and the tenderness in his hands, she grew jealous of that love, wanting some of it for herself, and saw Noldi's beauty, the beauty even of his bones as he grew closer to his skeleton, understood the miracle of that life that was in him, and, finally, loved him totally so that, when he went to his death, Ann understood that Elsa would go with him, crying that if to be a Jew was to be murdered, then she, too, was a Jew.

Every evening, the part of Ann that was a war bride cooked dinner, waiting for Herbie to praise it and for Marbella to remain indifferent to it, though not to Herbie, with whom she flirted outrageously, devouring him with her eyes while she devoured Ann's cooking with her strong white teeth. Herbie made a great show of suffering Marbella with gallant resignation, but Ann was so marginally present that she couldn't really care, and even later, after dinner, after the dishes, after the obligatory little social moments with Marbella, when she and Herbie could at last escape to bed to make love, she was often more Elsa than Ann. While they taught each other new pleasures, Ann was often overwhelmed by sadness for their doomed selves and for all those who were truly doomed, for whom such simple, natural delights were forever terminated. She would cry and Herbie would hold her and say, "There, there, post-coital *tristesse*, perfectly normal." And, in spite of herself, Ann would feel comforted.

"He's a real live wire," Major Donnely told her, slapping Herbie on the back. They were entertaining for the first time. "I hope you appreciate him, Mrs. Becker."

"Please call me Ann."

It was her birthday. She was twenty-two. Herbie had come home that evening weighed down with presents for her: the complete Beethoven quartets for the phonograph they had bought with some of the wedding present money, the Mozart piano concertos, a Billie Holiday album, two reams of typing paper, and, most remarkable of all, a typewriter. Where had the money come from? They were living on a staff-sergeant's pay, practically nothing.

"But I have a typewriter," she protested.

"That rickety little thing! That's okay for emergencies, for motel rooms, but this is a big sturdy machine that will sit on the desk like a rock and give you courage."

He was, really, adorable. "But the money, Herbie."

"I didn't actually buy it," he confessed. "It's G.I. I commandeered it for the duration."

"You stole it? Herbie, you'll be court-martialed."

"What the hell."

She pushed the potato chip dip and the walnut blue cheese balls across the coffee table, closer to the major and his pretty wife, Doreen, and further from Marbella, unavoidably also present, since she was part of the family. Marbella bit into one of the cheese balls and instantly spat it into a cocktail napkin with a gargle of disgust.

"Blue cheese," Ann said. "Surely you're no stranger to blue cheese, Marbella."

"I'm a stranger to it pressed this unexpected way between walnut halves. You must have spent the whole day engineering these things."

"Ah think they're delicious, Mz. Becker," Doreen said, a decent woman. "Ah'd ask for the recipe but ah think ah can figger it out."

"Please call me Ann."

Herbie, back from the bar they had improvised atop the console Philco, handed the major his replenished drink. Herbie had snatched the major's glass away from him before it was half empty. What a host! Marbella, the perfect guest, lazily extended her glass to Herbie and said, "Would you be a darling and get me a refill, too?"

"How long have you been married?" Ann asked Doreen, struggling desperately for conversation. Marriage was so much on her mind.

"Two years," Doreen said.

"Two years, imagine!" Ann said. "We've been married seven weeks."

"Tom passes so quickly," Doreen said. "And no, no children yet. Ah seem to find children inconceivable, ha, ha."

"Though not for want of trying," the major assured them, winking.

"Next week ahm havin' mah tubes blown."

"I'd gladly do it for her," the major said wickedly, "but the doctor tells me that's his job. Mine is to keep plugging away."

Ann cast wildly about for another topic. How would she ever get through this war! She had already ascertained that the Donnelys were from Memphis where he had left a successful advertising agency in the care of a partner with a perforated eardrum. The major and Doreen had been high school sweethearts. Doreen had given up college to marry him while she was still a high school senior, and had therefore not majored in any subject that could lend itself to discussion. Ann took a long swallow of her Scotch and thought about getting up to serve dinner.

"Have you been to our Art Institute?" Marbella, unexpectedly helpful, asked Doreen.

"Heah? In Dayton? Ah've been meanin' and meanin' to go, but truth to tell, ah haven't had a minute. What about you, Mz. Becker?"

"Ann. Call me Ann. A couple of times. What keeps you so busy, Doreen? Do you have a job?"

"Me? Whatever in the world would ah do?" she laughed. "Ah have no skills whatsoever."

The major interrupted what he had been saying to Herbie about tables of organization to wink again at Ann and say, "Don't you believe it."

"Well, ah do sew," Doreen said, blushing. "Ah sew all mah own clothing. Ah'd sew Burton's, too, but the U.S.A. gov'ment won't allow it."

Ann, who could barely thread a needle, was impressed.

"The dress you're wearing is lovely," Marbella said.

"Do you design them, too?" Ann asked.

"No, what you do, you buy the pattern? Buttericks?"

Ann, baffled by the question, was at a loss for an answer.

"But to tell the truth," Doreen went on, "what really keeps me busy is all the activities at the club. The officers' club? The wives are just the most active group, bridge tournaments and all. Do you play?" Her hand flew to her mouth and her face reddened. "Not that it matters, because you see, ah couldn't . . ."

The club was off limits to Ann, a mere staff sergeant's wife.

"Ah beg your pahdon," Doreen said with so much feeling that Ann began to like her. Her soft southern voice was so much pleasanter than Marbella's nasal midwestern twanging.

"It's all right, Doreen," Ann said, smiling as warmly as she could, meaning to comfort her. "In Europe they're burning babies." Doreen stared at her, startled. "What I mean," Ann said, "is it's not important." There was an odd noise inside her head, a sound like a distant scream. "I'd better go check on dinner."

The kitchen, little more than a jog in the hallway leading from the living room to the bedroom, nonetheless concealed her from their view and them from hers. She leaned her cheek against the cool refrigerator door and took deep breaths. The noise in her head subsided, then went away.

Dinner was stewing beef that she hoped she had transformed into a reasonable facsimile of beef stroganoff. Poverty, she was learning, required imagination and more time in the kitchen. She usually bought the daily special at the commissary if it was something she recognized. She was becoming a serious cook; after all, she was cooking not only for herself and her husband, but for the woman who coveted her husband.

She stabbed a piece of the meat with a fork; it was done. She had only to fold in the sour cream and toss chopped parsley onto the mounds of buttered noodles on which she hoped they would fill up. She also hoped there would be enough leftovers for tomorrow's dinner. Although she had begun to enjoy cooking, she was also discovering the oppressive regularity, the inevitability, with which evening arrived, dinner after dinner after dinner. It felt so good to be alone and out of the living room, away from the deadly small talk, that she did some useless clattering, killing time. Idly, she twirled a kitchen spoon around the inside of an empty pot, then saw that the major was standing behind her, watching. He was on his way to the toilet, and no wonder. "What you banging that empty pot for, honey?" he asked, putting an arm around her. "Hey, that looks almost as good as it smells."

"It's just about ready," she said angrily, because the major's hand had slid down to her ass, where it now lingered. There was nothing in his face to acknowledge what his hand was doing. If she hauled off and whacked him with the spoon, which she was dying to do, Herbie might be sent back to combat. Hell, she was in the army, too. "Why don't you just toddle along and do your wee-wee while I get this on the table?" she said.

He gave her a parting squeeze and continued on his way to the bathroom. But when they were gathered at the table and well into the meal, Ann became aware of the major's steady gaze on her.

"That boy of yours is going to go real far," he said, his eyes glinting. He had a loud, carrying voice. "Do you know that?"

"I hope you're right," she said.

"Of course he's right," Marbella said.

"My girls," Herbie said.

"He's got a mind that never stops," the major said. "Did you know that?"

"No," Ann said, genuinely surprised. "I didn't."

"Oh yes!" Marbella said. "And he's so funny. I giggle all day, remembering something he said at breakfast."

"He's a natural, this boy of yours."

"A real charmer," Marbella said.

"I always travel with my claque," Herbie said, modestly.

"I hope I can convince him to settle in Memphis after the war," the major persisted. "I want him on my team. How would you like to live in Memphis, Ann?"

"I don't know," Ann said. "It's something I don't recall ever thinking about."

"That's awfully nice of you," Marbella said to the major, smiling proudly.

"Because, Ann, there's a future in Memphis. Memphis is booming."

Who isn't, Ann thought. The only thing she knew about Memphis was that it was probably somewhere in Tennessee.

"And I'll take real good care of you," the major said. "The both of you."

When the endless evening finally ended, and doors had closed behind the Donnelys and Marbella, who vanished at once into her room out of range of the wreckage, Herbie piled the dishes in the sink where, against all her training, he persuaded her to leave them until morning. "It's your birthday," he reminded her.

She brushed her teeth, took two aspirin, and staggered into the bedroom. Herbie was in his undershorts, reaching into the closet for his pajamas. She watched him closely, seeing how his long, graceful body moved, the way veins appeared and muscles contracted and expanded beneath the firm fair skin with its overlay of fine golden hairs. In the simple act of reaching for the hook where his pajamas hung, and in the ordinary gesture required to remove the pajamas from the hook, there was a complexity that was startling and beautiful. For the first time, Ann understood that when he went out the door in the morning, he went *somewhere else,* to other places where he saw people, thought, spoke, performed acts, made choices and decisions, was seen, heard, judged. Some of those transactions he would report to her when he came home but, as witness the major's opinion of him, not all. A live wire, a young man who would go far, a mind that never stopped. She hadn't guessed any of this, nor even thought to guess it. She knew him to be kind and sweet and easy and safe, pleasing in the grace of his physical presence, and often funny. He never lost his temper, unlike her father who always did. She loved to look at him, to touch him, and she liked the sound of his voice, if not always the things he said. But what did she really know beyond that? What did she know of his true quality? How had they come to choose each other? It was a question she was unable to answer, and she was staggered by her carelessness. Please God, she prayed, let time prove me lucky. Luck was all.

She put her arms around him and spoke into the soft hollow at the base of his throat. "Did you marry me for my looks or my mind?" she asked.

"Neither. I married you for your money."

"What money? My father's money?"

"Yeah, your father has all the money. I'd have married your father but he was already married."

"How come you never say a serious word?"

"Here are four: dinner was a triumph."

"You already said that. Could we please never have another evening like this?"

"War is hell," he said.

"You already said that, too."

"And I'll go on saying it. War is always hell. Over and over and over."

SIX (now)

My father's pacemaker, a neat rectangle the size of a pocket calculator, has been implanted just beneath the skin, readily accessible. A simple procedure, not really an operation, but it's the first time he's been cut into in any way. His relief is mixed with indignation.

"Whew, he hurt me," he says repeatedly. "He really hurt me."

On the screen behind him, the paced heart makes neat and regular little triangular leaps from left to right, a rabbit's progress. A miracle. This man, who only a few years earlier would have died, is still hurting. A gadget has been invented to give him who knows how much more time, time in which to continue his habits and his personality.

"A miracle," my mother says, shaking her head in wonder.

"Technology," I say

The batteries should last two years before needing to be replaced. Meanwhile, my father will be provided with still another gadget to be used every Sunday night at seven o'clock, to connect his heartbeat to the telephone. His mechanical heartbeat will pulse across the wires to be checked by a machine on the other end. Why are people who slaughter one another in endless wars and so many other careless ways, also so ingenious about keeping themselves going?

And what does the pacemaker tell the heart? How does it do it, what is the stimulus and how does the heart know to respond? I could ask. I could easily look it up. But I won't. I want the mystery, the pale horse, pale rider, Atropos with her busy scissors, the angel, the summoner, Abraham's bosom --- not mechanical death, not death a wound-down machine.

My father has been moved from intensive care into a semi-private room. Mr. Ginsburgh, the man in the other bed, watches television from morning to night with the glazed eyes of a junkie. Not only drugged, he is also deaf.

"I hate that man," my father stage-whispers over the news. "He's driving me nuts."

"Why don't you get a private room?" I ask in all innocence, almost undoing the work of the doctors. He can certainly afford it.

"Do you have any idea how much more they cost?" he sputters, too weak to roar. Extravagance, unnecessary expense, never fail to raise his blood pressure, and both he and my mother have odd notions about what constitutes extravagance. My mother, who doesn't hesitate to spend thousands of dollars on her wardrobe, and whose jewels lie in a vault gathering value, can't bring herself to call a taxi. And my father, railing, is doomed to suffer Mr. Ginsburgh, whose leg has been amputated. In time, if Mr. Ginsburgh is given time, his stump will heal and he will be fitted with a prosthesis. Meanwhile, he lies hypnotized, entranced, transported, drugged, while before him the world, like my father's heart behind him, plays out its drama in the pale machineface: Mr. Ginsburgh's pale little face vis-à-televis. Like Angie, deep in her insomniac nights, her own face washed by the pale moon of all-night television.

"Everyone's asleep but me," she wrote in one of those final letters. "I'm watching stories. Everything is burning but Charlton Heston will save her, I'm sure of it. Everyone else has to dream their own stories but I can't sleep and this dark box is lit up and all these old stories packed inside it come out into our living room. What magic! I wish I could turn it on and you would come out into our living room. It's three o'clock in this long night. Why aren't you here?"

"The car's working all right?" my father asks. I'm still here, in Florida, to drive his car because of my mother's inability to call a taxi. He wants me to praise his Cadillac, which is four times larger than necessary, and whose hips sway like a strumpet's.

"Fine," I say. "It runs. It gets about eight miles to the gallon."

"Did you check the oil? The air in the tires?"

"Everything's shipshape."

"My daughter," he tells the private nurse, who has just returned from her lunch break. "Did you meet my daughter? She's a writer."

"You don't say? How do you do. Your father, he's some character, you could certainly put him in an article."

"That's what I tell her all the time. You want something to write about, write about me. I've had some life, from beginning to end, God forbid. But what she writes is mostly poems."

"Poems? Isn't that innaresting."

"Not to me, it's not interesting. If you have to write, I tell her, why not something the other person can read. Who reads poetry? Can't you get that sonofabitch to turn down the goddamn volume?"

Tick tock tick tock. His heart beats on. It's time to go. My mother and I will go to Pumpernick's for a corned beef on rye and a Celray, which they are no longer permitted to call Celery Tonic, probably because it's not tonic and there's no celery in it. There will be vats of pickles and sour kraut, a basket of delicious rolls that the waitress will put in a bag for us to take home to be reheated for breakfast tomorrow morning. After lunch we'll go to Publix, a vast, bright, musical supermarket, to pick up a few things. My mother will assume her no-nonsense marketing face, left over from another era when marketing was a one-on-one affair, mano a mano, you against the butcher, the baker, the fruit lady.

"After Publix," my mother tells me in the car, "we'll go to the Treasure Island mall. Flora told me there's a new dress shop, very à la modish, she says. We'll look in, see if they have anything interesting. Maybe something for you, Ann?"

"Thanks, I don't need anything."

"Why? You have so many dresses?"

I don't think I have any. I believe I gave the last one away a month ago to Blanche for her show in Boston. It's been at least a year since I've worn a dress and the requisite underpinnings: stockings, slip, bra.

"I don't wear them anymore," I say. "Where I live, I don't need them. Nobody wears them."

"You'll need a dress for the cocktail party."

"What cocktail party?"

"The one I'm giving as soon as Daddy is home. So you can meet him."

"Meet who?"

"You know who. Arthur Tannenbaum."

"Who's Arthur Tannenbaum?"

"You know very well, Ann. He's the man I want you to meet."

SEVEN: (Then)

Making a baby was the appropriate celebration of the end of the war, an offering to peace, to the now conceivable future. Herbie's and Ann's was a lovely pink boy named Nicholas after a forebear named Nathaniel who, Ann's father said, would not have appreciated the tribute.

"A saint's name," he said with disgust. "A name for Santa Claus. Certainly not a name for a Jewish boy."

It was the Russian association that appealed to Ann. Her Russian heritage, by which she meant Tolstoy, Dostoevsky, Chekhov, Pushkin, Turgenev, as well as her grandparents.

"First we were Jews," her father said. "Then Russians. But never really."

Now they were Americans and it wasn't a generation for Nathaniels. It would be the Nicks, Mikes, Kennys, Steves, Sharons, Ellens, who would grow up to embrace the more austere and dignified names for their own children, calling them Joshua, Jeremiah, Amanda, Deborah, Rebecca, Jessica.. Three syllable names, or more. The wheel would turn and turn again.

So it was Nicky Becker who lay upstairs, sleeping his way through infancy. Ann found him extraordinarily beautiful, especially his limbs, irresistible morsels for her to munch and nibble, savory, succulent, brand-fresh flesh already shaped to the promise of the man within. Had she really done this? *What had she done?* Her ecstasy was pierced with terror.

He was conceived on the day Herbie pinned on his ruptured duck, emblem of his "separation" from the service. They never dreamed it would instantly take. So many of the young wives they had come to know in Ohio, like Doreen, were keeping track of their temperatures and having their tubes blown, owing to a phenomenon that would later be termed Emotional Contraception. Who was Ann to anticipate instant fertility? How cocky it made Herbie, who took the credit as he would never have assumed the blame had it been otherwise.

She bore her burgeoning burden with pride and without complication, although she and Herbie were passing through difficult months readjusting to civilian life. Without a struggle, Herbie made the decision not to go back to school on the G.I. Bill and, instead, with money borrowed from Ann's father, opened an advertising agency with two friends from high school, one a commercial artist, the other the son of a manufacturer of garden implements, their first account. Since there were no apartments to be found, they moved into the new home of Ann's parents. Temporarily, they insisted. With twenty-five rooms, twice that number of acres, and a staff of five for house and grounds, Ann's parents were more than happy to have them; it made their consumption slightly less conspicuous. In fact, Ann's father rationalized buying the place because of the scarcity of apartments, knowing that it would long outlast the war's end. "You have to live somewhere," he said.

The estate was in Westchester on a high hill overlooking the Hudson River. He had bought it a year earlier while Ann and Herbie were still at war. His business was booming. It had survived the war and, unlike so much of the competition, the depression that preceded the war. Nonetheless, Ann's father was constantly fearful that the next season would bankrupt him, so that he had always been conservative about spending money, to the point of parsimony. But with the war's end in sight, with every prospect of increasing prosperity, he felt at the height of his powers, arrogant in his durability. It was no longer enough for him to know his own worth; he wanted it reflected in his lifestyle. When the real estate agent showed him Sleepy Hollow Acres, he bought it at once without even telling Ann's mother.

Herbie and Ann were home on furlough when he broke the news. It was spring. Through the dining room windows where they were having Sunday morning breakfast, they could see Central Park turning green and forsythia beginning to burst into golden bloom.

"We're going for a ride right after breakfast," Max said. "Get dressed."

"Herbie and I are going for a walk," Ann said. She wanted to be alone with Herbie, to talk to him. There had been a letter from Marbella, completely at odds with Herbie's version of their eviction from Marbella's apartment. Ann had come to New York a week earlier than Herbie. When he joined her, it was with the news that he had gone to the apartment one night to find all their bags packed and in the hall, the door locked, the locks changed, and a sheriff's notice on the door officially barring them from entry. It was, Herbie said, the vicious act of a woman scorned. It sounded entirely reasonable. What else could it have been?

"You're not going for a walk," her father said firmly. "We're going for a ride in the car. To the country."

"Where?" Ann's mother asked.

"You'll see."

"I don't want to go," Ann said. "I need some time alone with Herbie."

Marbella's letter was short and to the point. Herbie hadn't paid the rent for three months. She was sorry to have to do it. She wouldn't have minded waiting for the money a little longer, but despite Herbie's charming promises, she was convinced that his excuses were false, that he had no intention of paying what they owed. If Ann were wise, Marbella advised, she would assume the financial responsibility for their family. Herbie wasn't to be trusted.

"We were alone all night," Herbie reminded her. "I'd love to go for a drive in the country. It's a gorgeous day."

Marbella's letter had come two days ago. Ann's first reaction was to dismiss it as even more outrageous than the eviction itself. Marbella was jealous, a troublemaker. Ann crumpled the letter and tossed it into the wastebasket. Later, she retrieved it and put it in a drawer.

"What's the big mystery?" Ann's mother asked, but her question was addressed to Max, not to Ann.

"No big mystery, Polly," Max said, a faint quiver of excitement in his voice. "Just something I want you to see."

Ann sat in the back of the car with her mother, looking at the first blush of spring along the parkway, breathing the soft westerly air, feeling feverish and restless with that vague familiar longing that was almost nostalgia, that was spring fever, that she had imagined marriage and adulthood would have vanquished. There *had* been a little extra money in the past months. Herbie said his father had begun to send him a monthly check to help out. His business had picked up and it was the least he could do for a son who was serving his country. She had never actually seen those checks. Why would Herbie's father have sent them to the post instead of to their home address?

Oh, but it was unthinkable.

She stared at the back of Herbie's head. Her father was driving, Herbie was co-pilot. They turned off the parkway and headed west, toward the river. She loved the back of Herbie's head. It was perfectly shaped, his ears flat against it, the darkened gold hair curling to a point on his neck. How could a head like that hold secrets from her, or deception?

The car turned into a bluestone drive flanked by stone pillars which bore the carved words: SLEEPY HOLLOW ACRES.

"What is this?" Ann's mother asked nervously. "A country club? We already belong to a country club."

"It's not a country club, Polly."

"Some kind of institution? A school? A nursing home? A diet farm?"

"It's a house," Max said.

"What kind of house has a name?"

The drive wound up a hillside past a caretaker's cottage, greenhouses, barns, chicken coops, a freshly dug and planted vegetable garden the size of a baseball diamond, past a formal flower garden, a gazebo, a tennis court, garages. It came to a halt at the portal of a towering Norman castle, half-timbered stone, with gothic leaded-glass windows.

"Good God, Max," Ann's mother said, her voice filled with terror. "What the hell is that?"

He was out of the car, grinning, his fist full of keys. "You never saw a house before? Come on."

"What do you mean, come on?" she asked, hanging back.

But Max was already atop the stone steps, stabbing the massive oak door with a huge black key, causing it to fall away, groaning. They trooped behind him across the threshold and stood shivering in a wide entry hall, listening to the scurry of tiny feet.

"Mice," Ann's mother said in a doomed voice. "It feels like a mausoleum."

"Wait till you see it," Max said, his voice ringing through the hall, his color high, his hands shaking with excitement. "Come on!"

They followed, filing in and out of doorways, peering into spacious chilly rooms, Max redundantly naming them, like an agent trying to sell them the place, pointing out distinguishing features which he had memorized from his earlier inspection and from the brochure Mrs. Doolittle had had printed to assist in the sale of this mammoth white elephant. Nearly everything in the house had come from destroyed European chateaux and mansions of a multitude of periods: lintels, mantels, leaded glass, stained glass, sconces, chandeliers, architraves, archivolts, entablatures, ceilings, floors, marble, molding, fixtures. Paneling, floors, window sashes and trim were walnut, rosewood, mountain ash, teak, striped maple, mahogany, ebony; the variety of trees that had been murdered in the fashioning of this house was staggering, matched only by the variety of trees and shrubs, all of them what Max called "specimens," that throve outside on the surrounding, belonging acres. The house had three stories and a winding staircase that led from the third floor to a round tower room, almost entirely windowed, that gave onto a stone balcony. By the time they arrived there for the unimpeded view of the river ribboning twenty-odd miles south to the George Washington Bridge, clearly visible on this lovely day, they had passed through twenty-five rooms, only the five in the servants' wing less than grandiose, and eight bathrooms with bidets and silver fixtures.

"It's a hotel," Ann's mother said.

"It *is* a little ostentatious," Ann said, though she was beginning to feel excited. She was pretty sure why they were there.

"See? I'm not crazy," her mother said. "Forget it, Max. It's out of the question."

"In the question, out of the question, I already bought it."

There was a moment of shocked silence, and then Ann's mother moaned. "You bought it," she said in a small flat voice.

"I bought it."

"Oh, you fascist!" she muttered. Then, her voice rose, carrying over the balcony and across the sweep of lawn beneath them, and into the ring of trees beyond. "Without even asking me. I'm not even a junior partner in this so-called marriage!" Tears stood in her eyes. "Would you mind telling me one thing?" Her voice was now a scream. "Who the hell is going to dust it?"

Max laughed. Ann had never seen him so excited, so happy. "Come on, we'll go down to the swimming pool. Wait till you see it. Even in the movies you never saw anything like it."

This, then, was where they lived. An army of decorators swarmed through it for months with tape measures and swatches, transforming it, making it livable, warm, cheerful, soft underfoot with fields of sculptured broadloom. Ann and

Herbie and the baby had their own wing, two bedrooms with connecting bath, both bedrooms with fireplaces and French doors opening onto a balcony. By the time they moved in, she pregnant with Nicky, the episode with Marbella was almost forgotten. Herbie had told her in convincing detail of Marbella's attempted seduction the night following Ann's departure, and of his tactful and gentle, he had believed, failure to be seduced.

"I told her it was nothing personal," he said, smiling at the memory. "That I was flattered and that under ordinary circumstances I'd have liked nothing better, etcetera, but that I was a newlywed and still a little fond of my wife."

"Gee whiz," Ann said.

"There's not a lot you can say in a negative vein to a naked woman who is standing in the moonlight next to your bed that isn't going to upset her," he said. And of course he had paid the rent. He showed her the stubs in his checkbook. Later, when it occurred to her that she should have asked to see the cancelled checks instead, she felt like a monster for that lingering residue of mistrust. She put it out of her mind.

So Nicky lay asleep upstairs, a darling, a blessed miracle, perfect in every detail, a happy baby, a smiler and gurgler, all promise, innocent and pure, her baby boy, the first grandchild on either side of the family. He and Sleepy Hollow Acres, particularly its swimming pool, provided a host of aunts, uncles, cousins, brothers, sisters, parents and grandparents, their wives, husbands, children, friends, with an excuse to take the car out of the garage on a sunny day. The Olympic-sized pool was built into a flowering hillside down which an artificially created waterfall meandered, circulating and purifying the pool's water. At its shallow end, the pool had been extended into the hillside to form a small echoing blue grotto. There were twin stone bathhouses. The pool was bordered by a wide swathe of flagstones, among which were planted mulberry trees, crabbed and oriental. Sun worshippers draped the poolside from mid-May until the first real frost, a long season.

Most of their guests arrived uninvited and unheralded. They appeared at the crest of the hill, shaded by a magnificent copper beech tree, then slowly descended into the sunlight via the steep, perilous stone steps, while below, the family looked up and tried to guess who they were.

"Herbie, go see if they have tickets," Ann's mother said, glancing up from her card game. Her own friends were always present in sufficient numbers to keep the canasta game going throughout the summer. Sometimes the arrivals were relatives, often distant, of the Silvers, but more and more often they belonged to Herbie's family. Herbie also had new people to impress, prospective clients, and he had had maps printed, while Ann, who had become active in postwar politics, had made new friends at meetings, well-to-do local revolutionaries and intellectuals, who had also begun to pay calls, sometimes on horseback. One of these, Alexander Steiner, a stylish Viennese refugee, entirely oblivious of Herbie, was courting Ann. Ann's callers were usually identifiable by their white costumes, since they rarely used the swimming pool without first warming up on the tennis court. The two figures descending on this sunny Saturday, the first of the day's callers, were not dressed in white.

"That might be my Uncle Jacob," Herbie said, squinting up from the layout of an ad he was working on for the Karger Weed-Gouger. Beneath an illustration of the implement, and of a cornucopia of vegetables and flowers, Ann winced to see the copy, which read: "WEED 'EM AND REAP."

"That's not your Aunt Rose," she said.

"It's Uncle Jacob, all right. My God, that must be his mistress."

Herbie's Uncle Jacob was only one of several family black sheep, a drinker, gambler and philanderer, with a wife who never smiled. Ann sometimes wondered if it was his ways that had soured her or hers that had turned him rakish, or if they had both been what they were from the start, attracted to each other out of a need to justify their natures.

They watched Jacob and the woman make the slow, tortuous descent. He could hardly be sober even this early in the day, Ann reasoned, if he was bringing them his mistress. She watched each step with held breath. As they neared the bottom, Ann's father threw down the newspaper he'd been reading and said, "I've had enough, God damn it," and, thrusting out his jaw, he rose from the chaise where he had been sunning himself and strode to the foot of the path. What he said, inaudible to the rest of them, turned the visitors smartly around in their tracks. Before they had touched down, they were climbing back up.

"Drunks and whores," Max muttered angrily as he marched back. "A man's home is his castle, even when it *is* a castle."

Uncle Jacob and his paramour were halfway up the hill, she now in the lead, when she stopped abruptly and, wheeling to face them, raised a fist and screamed, "Down with the nouveau riche and their disgusting manners!" The woman's vehemence, or perhaps the sheer force of her breath, caused Jacob to stagger and lose his footing. His arms churned as he slid crazily down the hill, landing in a silent heap at the foot of the steps. Above him, the woman screamed and screamed. Herbie was the first to leap up and run to where his uncle lay. Alarmed, Ann and her parents followed.

"He's dead, you bastard," the woman howled from her perch. "His blood is on your head."

Jacob stirred, groaning, and tried to struggle to his feet while Herbie knelt to help him.

"Are you hurt, Uncle Jacob?"

"Dead, dead, dead. Murderers!"

"Quiet!" Uncle Jacob gasped. "I am not dead, but I think I may be broken."

"I knew it," she screamed at Jacob, beginning to grope her way back down. "I should have listened to the I Ching instead of to you. Idiot!" She teetered on her high heels. Ann ran to catch her and brought her safely down. "The I Ching," she told Ann, "said, 'The confidence symbolized by power in the toes is soon exhausted.' I ask you, could it have been any clearer?"

"Where does it hurt, Uncle Jacob?" Herbie asked.

"Christ," Ann's father muttered between his teeth.

"The left leg. Ahhh."

"Christ," Max swore again. "Drunks, whores, crazies, and now, God forbid, litigation."

"I am so sorry," Jacob said, grimacing in an effort to smile. "At our age, I'm afraid, we tend to fall down more."

"And stand up less," the woman said, laughing hysterically.

"Forgive me, I have not introduced you," Jacob said, his face contorted with pain. "Please, may I present my friend, Countess Tanya Melnikoff."

"How do you do?" Herbie said politely. Ann, attempting a smile, heard an odd clicking inside her head, as though a camera there had snapped a picture she must never forget. It was a loud click, sharp and startling.

"We have to get out of here, Herbie," she heard herself thinking. She had been saying it to him more and more often.

"I'm going up to call an ambulance, Uncle Jake," Herbie said. "Just lie quietly until they come. I'll get a cushion for your head."

"I'll get it," Ann's mother said. "You go."

They watched Herbie bound up the stone hillside and disappear. The countess began to moan.

"What about me?" she said, wringing her hands. "Why has no one the sense at least to offer me something to drink?" Tall and thin, almost gaunt, the hands the countess was wringing, Ann noticed, were small and blunt with prominent blue-green veins and short, carelessly bitten nails. Ann peered at her face, wondering if she was really a countess.

"I'll get you a drink, Tanya," she said. The countess removed the large purple sunglasses that had concealed most of her face, and turned her small green eyes, full of anger and shrewdness, toward Ann. The mouth she had painted over her thin lips was a bruise, a crimson smear, and her bright red hair had been teased to look as though the wind had permanently caught it, but her nose, too small for the bones of her face and lightly peppered with freckles, made the countess look like a ruined waif.

"Come," Ann said, frightened, taking the countess's arm. "We'll go up to the house for that drink."

"Up and down, up and down," the countess said, preceding Ann with alacrity. "I feel like, what is that child's toy? A yo-yo."

"I'm so sorry this had to happen," Ann said.

"Had to happen? It did not have to happen. It was not predestined. There is still cause and effect. The effect we begin to know, though I suspect we have only the beginning of it. As for the cause, the cause is your father's disgusting rudeness."

"Yes," Ann said, again hearing the click in her head. "Watch that next step, it's loose. My father thinks he's a moral man, but he's only prudish. His abstract thinking is so simple that it often makes him violent."

Ann felt the tension go out of the arm she held. Her own arm stiffened, almost reflexively, as if the tension had flowed like transfused blood from the countess to her. They reached the top of the hill and stood beneath the copper beech tree while the countess regained her breath. The broad lawn stretched before them toward the house that, with the sun on it, rose like a pink mirage from some fairy tale. How clear and blue the sky was, how golden green the sunlit lawn, how dappled cool the shade where they stood breathing, regarding each other, Ann and this peculiar woman. How peaceful and absurd.

The countess sighed as they began to cross the lawn. "A place like this," she said, "it is extremely seductive. But you mustn't go on living here. Why does your husband permit it?"

"The housing shortage," Ann said, surprised. What did the countess know? "Are you really a countess?"

"Of course! That is, I am an "if" countess. If this had not happened, and if that had happened as it was meant to, then I would have been a countess. The revolution. But in all fairness, and in my blood, I am a countess. What is that?"

It was a large brown horse trotting toward them, Alexander Steiner astride. Across the lawn. Her father would have a fit. It was a handsome horse and as it crossed the lawn, its beautiful black tail arched high, it sowed in its wake, like a trail of punctuation, a row of steaming golden turds.

"It's a horse," Ann said. "His name is Lothar."

"I know a horse when I see a horse," the countess said irritably. "Don't I spend half my life at the track with that fool Jacob? The question is rhetorical. Why is that horse on the lawn, and trotting straight at us?"

Alexander, natty in jodhpurs and yellow polo shirt, a figured blue bandana knotted at his throat, reined the horse to a stop a few yards short of them and slid gracefully from the saddle.

"Look what you've done to the lawn," Ann shouted, really angry. "My father will be furious!"

"Strictly speaking, I did not do it to the lawn," Alexander said in his careful English, smiling patiently at her. "The horse did it to the lawn. What the horse did to the lawn is good for the lawn. It will nurture it."

"That lawn has all the nurturing it needs," Ann said. Then, remembering her manners, she introduced the countess. Alex bowed, smiling his dazzling white smile.

"Are we never to have that drink?" the countess muttered from behind the huge sunglasses.

"We're on our way to the house for a drink," Ann explained to Alex, noticing that the beautiful lawn had begun to tilt. She reached for the countess's arm to keep from falling.

"Isn't it a little early in the day?" Alex said, glancing at his watch.

"Yes," Ann said, feeling a rising nausea.

"I will accompany you, if I may. I must, you see, talk to you, Ann."

"You can't talk to me, Alex," she said as he fell into step beside them, leading Lothar. The lawn was definitely undulating beneath her feet. Was it an earthquake? Neither Alex nor the countess seemed to notice. As the lawn rose and fell, Ann had difficulty knowing how to place her feet.

"Why not?" Alex asked. "Why can't I talk to you?"

"Because we don't have a subject."

He laughed merrily. "We could hardly have a better one," he said. "I was awake most of the night thinking about that subject."

Ann had never been able to ask him how he and his mother had managed to escape, and with all that money. The remainder of his family, as far as he knew, were ashes. Now, inexplicably, she urgently wanted to ask him.

"There's another reason," she said, her voice thickening in her mouth.

"What?"

But she had forgotten. He turned to peer at her, concerned. She was overcome by dizziness and nausea and fear. She stumbled and nearly fell.

"What is it, my darling?" he said, grabbing her free arm. "You're so pale. Are you ill?"

She was falling off the side of the earth, spinning in space. Why then was the countess looking at her with that inappropriate expression on her face, looking from Alex to her? "Please, countess . . ." she mumbled.

"Tanya. Do not call me countess."

"Please, Tanya, go into the house and ask anyone you see to show you to the bar and to bring ice."

The countess, who had already had enough trauma for one day, and had no interest left for whatever was ailing Ann, left them. They could hear the rising scream of a siren. It was tolling for Jacob, not for her.

"What is it, Alex?" she said, disintegrating. "What is it?" He folded her in his arms and, stumbling, half carried her toward the house.

"Too much sun, perhaps," he said, worried. It was still morning, and cool. "It will be better in a moment. You will lie down and I will bathe your brow, your eyes, your wrists, my beloved, and it will soon pass, I promise you, my darling, how your heart is beating, do not be afraid."

She was oddly comforted by his words and by his strong arms, and by the pungent smell of the horse trotting alongside them, though Alex had dropped the reins. As they neared the veranda, Herbie and two white-clad men streaked past. Herbie wheeled, waving the men on ahead, and ran back, blocking their path.

"Take your hands off my wife, Alex," he said.

"Get out of the way, Herbert," Alex said.

"Oh, Christ," Ann said, wrenching free of them both and managing, somehow, to make it to the house and up the stairs and into the cool, cool bathroom where she locked the door and lay down gripping the spinning floor, her cheek pressed to the cold white tile. After a while, above the drumming of her heart and the roaring in her ears, she heard from the adjacent room the small, not yet urgent sounds of Nicky

Nicky waking from his nap. He would need his diaper changed. He would be hungry. Oh, God, she thought, who would take care of him? Who would take care of her? Soon, Nicky, not yet, in a minute. She'd figure out what was happening to her, this, was it panic? She'd pull herself together. She'd stop things turning, falling. She would make her heart go slower. And be Nicky's mother. She would do the things that mothers do.

EIGHT: (now)

"Why are you sitting there like that?" my mother asks.

"Like what?"

"In a trance."

I'm at my father's desk, going through the stack of mail that has piled up on it, none of it, as Angie would say, "friendly." It all has to do with money, buying and selling, getting and spending, winning and losing. Bored, my mind has strayed.

"I'm thinking."

"What about?"

"His shirts."

I shuffle through the envelopes. My father has asked me to see if anything has come from Mishkin, O'Brien, Gallagher and Saperstein, his attorneys.

"What about his shirts?"

"Has he ever had one that wasn't monogrammed?"

"Not within memory. So?"

"He always wore his initials over his heart. Even on his pajamas. 'Personalized,' he called it."

"Why are you talking about him in the past tense?"

"Now he'll be personalized over a machine."

"All the more reason," my mother says. As usual, she is smoking.

The heart beating. The heart's handy helper, a machine, without which nothing. The monogram, his identity, his ego. What a sandwich!

"Here it is," I say, tearing open the envelope. As my father feared, the re-negotiation of the Arkmore mortgage is inadvisable at this time owing to a recent rise in interest rates, now one half of one percent too high. It is all virtually meaningless to me, but in actual fact, my father told me, $320,000 of real money, all profit, will not be realized. Now that his heart is again working, he'll be disappointed.

"He's not going to like it," I say.

"Then we won't bring it to the hospital. It can wait."

"He doesn't seem to think so."

"What if he had died?"

Just what I had been thinking. "He's the kind of man who'll never die with all the loose ends tied up. All those deals, investments, mortgages, property, stocks, bonds, notes, options, puts and calls."

My mother laughs. "What do you know about puts and calls?"

"The Value Line Newsletter will keep on coming and coming, moaning to his ghost."

"Why so morbid?"

The smell of her cigarette fills me with the anguish of desire, a palpable yearning, a nostalgia I taste in my mouth, my throat, my nose, my lungs, a devastating deprivation that makes me cranky. "I'm not morbid. I woke up depressed." A bad dream. "Something I dreamed," I say, remembering. "It opened with a title, like a movie."

"Don't tell me. I hate it when people tell their dreams."

The title was in French. "Hommes de la Cité." An endlessly complicated dream, or so it seemed in the dreaming, with a cast of thousands. Jed and Nick were in it, and Angie was in and out of it, once disguised as an astronaut. But it was the title that intrigued. What could it mean?

The telephone rings, as it has been doing intermittently all morning. Well-wishers. There are five telephones in the apartment, two of them here in the study area. The green one on the desk is my father's, strictly for business, with its own number, tax-deductible. The pink princess phone is at my mother's elbow next to an ashtray, already almost full, along with her jeweled eyeglass case, on the fruitwood end table beneath a lamp that provides light for her to read by at night when she's not watching television on the 26-inch color set centered in the entertainment console opposite the reclining, though not at this moment reclined, chair in which she sits smoking and doing the daily crossword puzzle between phone calls.

I sit on, not listening to the one-sided conversation which doesn't vary sufficiently from the earlier ones to divert me from my increasing malaise and restlessness. I feel the way I usually do when I sit down at my desk to write. For at least one fleeting moment, I invariably wish I were a singer instead of a writer. Elizabeth Schwarzkopf. Those glorious sounds coming out of me. My mouth. Instead of waiting, mouth shut on a dark and silent place, for words to travel down some dim back stairway into my hands, I would think a note, open my mouth to shape it, and send it forth like a brilliantly colored butterfly, a glorious pure and thrilling sound whose only meaning is itself. Nothing between it and me but my breath. Nothing between notion and execution but trained volition. If I believed in God, it would be because of such gifts, so arbitrarily bestowed.

"That was Arthur," my mother says, hanging up.

"Arthur?"

"Arthur Tannenbaum. He called to ask about Daddy. He says he's looking forward to meeting you."

"I'm going for a swim."

"Good."

She is proprietary, as if it were her ocean, her climate, her sunshine, happy when I use the facilities.

"Why don't you come, too?" I ask. She's a good swimmer. She can swim great distances, doing an effortless breast stroke. She sometimes talks about wanting to die that way, if she ever loses her marbles, swimming out into the sunset. Of course, if she loses her marbles, she'll forget swimming. She'll never think of suicide.

"I just had my hair done."

"Wear a cap."

"It gets wet anyway."

"So when can you swim?"

She has had a standing beauty parlor appointment at nine o'clock every Friday morning.

"Thursday afternoons," she says. "If I don't have a dinner date. Or very early Friday morning."

I leave her for the guest bedroom, mine for the duration of my stay, which is now in its fourth day. Already, I've fallen out of the pattern of my own life and into that of my mother's. I pull my bathing suit out of a drawer and change into it, then stand at the window looking out at the ocean, so temperamentally and physically unlike its northern counterpart. I listen hard, but all I can hear is the faint hum of the air-conditioning. Raising the aluminum-framed window, surprised to find that it opens, I immediately feel the heat of the sun-conditioned outside air, and breathe the smell of the sea and the sun. For a while, I listen to the ocean lapping against the thin strip of beach that has been spared by developers, and not yet claimed by the sea. Two pure white gulls circle effortlessly, beautifully, against the cloudless blue sky.

But why was Angie disguised as an astronaut? Oh, of course! The first time I saw her was in the pavilion near the swimming pool. She had rented a color television set --- color was a relatively recent innovation, an expensive luxury --- so that we could all watch the first moon walk. She'd thought it important to watch something so momentous in color, not realizing that there would be no color on the dead moon, that the astronauts would be ghosts in white shrouds moving like zombies on the barren, cold, gray moonface. It was a bright July day, not unlike this one, at an artists' colony in the Green Mountains. I was there for the first time, high on the honor of having been admitted, and of finding myself among writers and painters and composers, instead of psychiatrists and advertising people and social workers. I was working hard, writing almost all the poems in Taking Sides, euphorically in love with myself, as I'd never been before, and with everyone else there where, at least for a little while, I felt as if I knew exactly who I was. I'd never been happier.

Angie had arrived only that morning. When she came into the pavilion, she didn't smile or greet anyone. She sat on the floor in a corner near the television set, her chin on her knees, her arms clasping her legs, a vertical foetal position. I couldn't take my eyes off her, not because she was beautiful. She wasn't. She had a thin, pale face, reamed with intelligence, and with something else, suffering or pain. Her hair was yellow and spiky, straight, unmanageable, cowlicky hair. Later, I'd see other things, the stubborn chin, the once-dimpled cheeks, now vertically cleft, the firm upper lip opposed to the unexpectedly full, almost dissolute lower lip, the smile, when it was finally allowed to appear, that shattered her face into a new arrangement of unexpectedly dazzling facets. Her soft, beautiful voice. Her catlike grace. Her funny child's hands. The back of her neck, so vulnerable.

When, that first day, she gradually noticed me staring at her, she scowled, her eyes so blue, so deep, that I had the feeling that I could drown in them. The scowl amused me. I could see the child she must have been, a thin and silent golden waif, quirky with genius and anger, and I knew then that Angie was going to be in my life, and crucial. I also knew that she knew it, that we were instantly alive to each other. Some enchanted evening, I thought. Frightened, I looked away, concentrating on the TV screen.

For the first time, humans stood on land that wasn't of this earth, robbing the moon of its mystery. They planted a flag on it and took golf swings, and picked up rocks, and so much for the romantic hollow-eyed man in the moon. I think it was then that I knew I was going to leave Herbie. I was ready. My new poems. New friends. The moon. Maybe Angie.

The emotion of those first days returns to me now in a rush of memory. Where, I wonder, does all the feeling go when it goes? Maybe to that barren, lonely moon, there to howl and moan, an eternal wind among the dead rocks. How much better there than in the cul-de-sac of my heart, where it's been trapped far too long. How stupid and crippled it makes me feel! Will it never go away?

I put on the beach coat and sandals my mother bought for me the day after my arrival, having ascertained that I wasn't suitably equipped to negotiate the sojourn from Penthouse W down the long hall, into the elevator where I press BEACH, out again through the rear lobby, past the kidney-shaped swimming pool with its surround of chaises and baking bodies, past the shuffleboard court and the putting green and down the short wooden stairway onto the tiny strip of sand where I slip off the beach coat and sandals and ease myself upon the empty sea there to float, gently rocking, eyes closed, mind lulled.

After some moments of mindless peace, it comes to me, with a shudder of disgust, that I've dreamed, not for the first time, an incredibly awful, probably irrelevant pun, that Hommes de la Cité translates, oh so roughly, into the word 'mendacity.'

NINE (then)

    Catapulted from sleep into the black void of night and her terror, Ann sat bolt upright, feeling that she was about to die, that the Thing inside, the Thing that was going to kill her, was traveling from her head to her chest and, in a moment, would reach her heart, her center, and explode.

    She listened intently. Within the roaring of her panic were smaller sounds, a grinding and creaking in her head, a tightening in her chest, the wild thump of her heart. Now, she thought. Now and now and now and NO! Not yet not now. Fear curled around her gutless guts, clutched her racketing heart. Here was death within her, now and here and with this next breath, and Goddamn, she was only twenty-five; the doctors couldn't find anything wrong with her.   In the adjoining room, Nicky slept. Beside her, Herbie slept. Deeply. Across the hall, hugged in the Chinese Chippendale embrace of the master suite, her parents slept. In other rooms, since it was a weekend, guests slept, and beyond, in their separate wing, servants slept. Only Ann was awake in the inky night, vibrant with panic, isolated by the mystery and privacy of her struggle, exhausted not into but out of sleep by the effort of being who she was: nobody, all body.

    It was too dark. She couldn't fight death in its own arena, the everywhere-dark. Fumbling, she switched on the bedside lamp. Out of the shadows the night-extinguished room dutifully sprang. Faithfully there the darkly polished spoolbedposts, the graceful little table with its gleaming brass candlestick holder, the Dutch-tiled fireplace, the pale green wallpaper with its tiny geometric figure, the soft darker green of the carpet upon which all the rest sat as in a garden. The lovely, lovely room in which she lay, rigid and sick with fear, waiting for death to snuff out her wildly pounding heart. What is it, what is it, what is it?

Herbie, beautiful in sleep, stirred and groaned, then opened his eyes and stared stupidly at her. "Damn," he said, raising up on an elbow, his eyes unglazing. "Whassa matter, honey, you dying again?"

She nodded, ashamed, her eyes filling with tears. She tried to speak but her mouth was too dry, her teeth too tightly clamped. It was cold, cold, cold, and she began to shiver uncontrollably. He put an arm around her, trying to fold her into his warmth, but she lurched free.

"Don't!" she said. If she relaxed for an instant, It would have her.

He sighed. "You want a pill?"

She stared straight ahead. The cold had unlocked her teeth and set them to chattering. A pill.

He padded into the bathroom and returned with a glass of water and one of the precious bullet-shaped capsules. She looked at it, cushioned in the palm of his extended hand, so brightly colored, so cleverly contrived, such a small and foolproof avenue of escape. She took it in fingers she couldn't hold steady and somehow got it into her mouth and down, gagging. At once, conditioned, she began to relax. Slowly, she prepared herself for this invited welcome death, so unlike the terrible one she was for the moment eluding.

"Science," she said, glancing at the bedside clock. Half-past three. In five minutes she'd be drunk. In ten she'd be floating on a soft warm cloud. In another five she'd be safely asleep. "Give me a cigarette, please."

He lit two, putting them both in his mouth in a deliberately awkward imitation of some movie character, looking not sexy but fanged.

"Could you just give me a cigarette," she said. "without getting it all spitty?"

A shadow flew across his face. "You believe wan of these smooks was for you, cherie? Ha!" He arched an eyebrow and puffed vigorously at both cigarettes, a dense cloud of smoke wreathing his face. "Eet ees I am heavy smookair, ze nex' thing to chain smookair, gang smookair." Fumbling, he added a third cigarette to his mouth, but she snatched it away before he could light it, almost able to laugh. The cold was thawing. Slowly, tentatively, she leaned into the pillows, the muscles in her back aching from tension.

"Annie, Annie. If you could see yourself." He was sitting on the edge of the bed, facing her, and he took one of her hands and held it. "You look ten years old, a little girl who's seen a ghost."

"Exactly."

"Your hair's standing straight up."

She had been running a hand ceaselessly through her hair, pressing against her scalp into the brain where the rotting was happening. Gently, he stroked her hair back into place. "We could make love," he said, "if you were going to be around long enough."

"Jesus, Herbie!"

"But there are some things you need help with."

"I believe that." Her speech was beginning to slur. "There are one or two things you can't do by yourself. Tango. Ping-pong. Quarrel." Wrong, you could quarrel.

He yawned. She saw that in spite of his concern and tenderness, he was eager to get back to sleep. She thought about bringing it up again, about how they ought to get out of this Wuthering Heights setting and into something of their own. She knew what he'd say. "Soon. Give me a chance to get started. I'm just getting on my feet." She'd accuse him of liking it here and he'd say, "What's not to like?" But, really, it no longer mattered because her body was sinking into the soft comfort of the bed, embraced by it. The air was that of a cool, lovely summer night, not the damp, cold, smothering air of hell. "If I could just get through to you," she mumbled, not for the first time. "Really feel you there."

"I'm here all right," he said, grinding out his cigarette in the delicate Delft ashtray provided by the management. "The failure is in your feelers." He took the cigarette from between her fingers. "You're about to go."

"If only you weren't so gorgeous," she mumbled.

When she awoke, battered and groggy, she could see by the position of the sun's reflection in the river that the day, bright and clear, was well advanced. The river sparkled and, beyond, Nyack lay clean and snug in its hillside.

Herbie was gone. She could hear sounds of activity outside, sounds of the place being maintained and improved. Almost always, there was the whirring of a motor, the drone of grass being cut, dead limbs pruned, the topography rearranged. It was Saturday, her father's big day, when he increased the outside staff from two to half a dozen, moving the men about like chess pieces, barking orders, supervising, mopping sweat from his brow as though he himself were laboring, though his function was strictly executive, the foreman. He had never been a physical man. An executive all week in his factory, he was an executive all weekend at home. Here, as there, motors hummed.

The rich smell of baking rose from below and drifted under the bedroom door, poignantly reminding her of how lovely hunger used to be. Swedish coffee cake. Huge golden apple pies. Steaming crusty loaves of bread.

Reluctantly, she quit the bed and, through the French doors that opened onto the balcony, stepped into the day. Here, too, the air was delicious; it would be impossible to choose between the smell of baking and that of newly cut grass. Across the lawn, beneath the huge somber copper beech where the path led up from the pool, Herbie gradually appeared, carrying Nicky. There were only the two heads at first, then the rest of them emerged from the shadows into the full sunlight. They were in swimming trunks and Herbie's yellow hair was matted flat. Holding the baby high, he did a little dance, and Ann knew exactly how the grass felt beneath his feet, and the sun on his arms. She knew, although she couldn't hear, that he was singing some kind of nonsense song to Nicky and that deep in his throat Nicky was gurgling with happiness. Every so often, to accent the beat, Herbie kissed the exact center of Nicky's fat round belly. She felt that she was seeing them impersonally, objectively, like a tourist in a strange country, entirely unconnected and superfluous. She had been a middleman, a most unlikely vessel through which the world had renewed itself. If she died, her death would alter nothing.

So the coffee cakes baked, the grounds were clipped and swept, the child was loved and would prosper. Beyond the far side of the house, past the flower garden, the tomatoes ripened in the sun and the corn tassels were browning. Yesterday, they had rolled the tennis court and repainted its lines. Below, in the swimming pool, the algae-free water circulated and re-circulated, freshening itself as if it were precious as blood. Beside the pool, from time to time, a fat ripe mulberry fatly plopped onto the flagstone.

It was another day, a day that stretched endlessly ahead. How was she going to get through it?

She would lie on the water and the water would rock her and she would think absolutely nothing and she would look up at the sky and it would calm her and she would pass in and out of dreams remembering nothing knowing nothing and time would pass and perhaps a magic would happen and she would rise up pure, new and healed.

She felt the impact of Herbie's body hitting the water. The rubber raft on which she lay (how long? hours? days?) gave a sudden, storm-tossed lurch. Her eyes opened on a spray of flying sun-struck diamonds. It was Herbie's usual dive, imperfect, but loaded with zest. He plowed through the water like a seal at herring time. When he reached her side, he rested his chin on the raft, inches from her face.

"You'll get flabby lying around like this all day," he said. She'd lost fifteen pounds. Her bones showed. "It crossed my mind that maybe you could do with a little something to eat, seeing as how you missed lunch. And breakfast."

"I'm a cloud. Clouds don't eat lunch."

"I could bring it to you on a tray, balanced on my head. You'd hardly have to move."

"This is uxory, Herbie."

"A tidbit. A morsel. A pizza. A corned beef on rye, with a big fat full-sour pickle, the kind you love."

"Thanks anyway, Herbie, but please go away. You're interrupting."

He wasn't really worried about her. All the doctors agreed that there was nothing, nothing the matter with her.

"Your mother says you're wasting away. She thinks it's my fault, that I'm neglecting you in some important way. Financially. Sexually."

"I'll disabuse her."

"Even the countess. She said, 'Herbie, go out to your wife and puncture her apathy.' She talks dirty."

"Is she here again?" Her eyes swept the three sides of the pool where the bodies were draped in various attitudes of relaxation and sun-worship. Yes, there was Tanya, sprawled on a chaise, fingers drooping a hair's breadth from the eternal gin and tonic.

"She never left," Herbie said. "She sleeps in the bath house, upright in the shower."

Ann's mother had offered the countess one of the guest rooms for a few days after Jacob's fall so that she could take care of him while he was in the local hospital, a well-meant but stupid error, since Jacob's wife quite naturally appeared, bitterly dutiful.

"The final straw," she had told Jacob. "I'm throwing you out, body and soul."

"How can you throw me out when I'm lying helpless?" Jacob wearily responded.

"That one I can certainly throw out!" she said, rounding on Tanya. The countess vacated her room and departed for a while, but she had been reappearing at intervals without explanation, as though certain rights had been conferred because of the indignities she had suffered. She simply materialized, smiling wanly, changed her clothes in the bath house, helped herself to drinks from the poolside bar, took her place in the sun, then vanished again some hours later when the sun was close to the horizon.

Not far from where she now lounged, Ann's mother sat playing cards with three of her cronies beneath a gaily fringed umbrella angled against the sun. They played a complicated game requiring an enormous number of cards, and the women, in their damp and fashionable bathing suits, played with fierce concentration. Beyond them, Moe and Solly Shapiro, tax-deductible guests from Ann's father's real world, played gin rummy, sweat beading their naked skulls, fat cigars gripped between stubby fingers. A few yards further, beneath a mulberry tree, Nicky slobbered in his playpen, intently struggling to grow teeth and to teach himself to stand. She watched him, feeling so much love and pain that tears filled her eyes. He was still so new, yet so certainly there! Earlier, she had given him his lunch, changed his diaper, hugged and kissed him all over and tried to sing him into his nap. But her off-key voice had kept him amused and awake, and she had sat silent for a while, watching him fall asleep, then slipped away. There was so little for her to do, but it took all her energy to keep the earth from wobbling and the trees from falling down; to keep the terror, the enemy, at bay.

Herbie, his chin still resting on the raft, was looking into her eyes out of Nicky's eyes, waiting, she had forgotten why.

"Go talk to Alex," she said. "He's lonely."

"He's reading," Herbie said sullenly.

"He's only reading because he hasn't got anyone to talk to."

"He's deeply engrossed. He's reading Freud's love letters to his mother."

"Talk to him anyway. He thinks you have no conversation."

"He said that? To you? The fucker." He gargled water deep in his throat, then sent a jet squirting straight up in the air and plunged into a backstroke, leaving Ann to concentrate on the hillside at the unpeopled end of the pool. She closed her eyes and drifted, half dozing. ". . . these panics," she heard Herbie say to Alex. "She really believes she's dying, I don't know why." She paddled out of range of their voices, eager not to hear Alex's thoughtful, Freudian response. He was such an authority on so many subjects, not the least of them Love.

At a safe enough distance, she opened her eyes. Alex's profile was bent in aquiline intensity over the words he was saying to Herbie, whose existence he had gradually and reluctantly been forced to acknowledge. She could imagine what he was saying. Love of death love of life fear of death fear of life love fear fear love death life life death boomlay boomlay boomlay blah.

His hands, commuting between his lap and the arms of his chair, made subtle, expressive gestures that she might have missed if she had been listening to his words. Fascinated, she watched his hands living their separate articulate life, beautiful hands sculpting thought. For the first time, it struck her that perhaps she would have an affair with him, after all.

His hands fluttered still and came to rest in his lap. He had stopped talking. Beneath his European haircut, a pulse throbbed visibly. She wondered if he was having one of his migraines. But no, from his small, wry smile, she knew that he had stopped talking in the middle of a sentence, having noticed that as usual Herbie wasn't listening to him. Herbie, looking off into space, wore his glazed, anaesthetized look. She was embarrassed for him. She would have given anything to know where he went when his attention wandered, as it so easily did, and if, indeed, he went anywhere at all.

She turned again to the hillside and caught sight of her father, about to descend the irregular stone steps that led from the lawn above. He paused at the summit to survey the cluttered panorama below. His was the unmistakable stance of the conqueror, ownership aggressively marking the thrust of his jaw, the set of his shoulders. Despite what must have been the sweetness of this moment of dominion, the expression on his face was sour. His reaction to this place, this symbol of his triumph, was far from unmixed. Nothing would ever satisfy him, no one would ever really please him, nothing could ever measure up.

Her eye was caught by a pale, bobbing thing floating on the surface of the water a few feet from her. Unable to make out what it was, she paddled closer, reaching for it. Twice it eluded her and only when her hand closed on it did she realize with a lurch of fear that what she held was a glob of sponge rubber molded into the shape of a woman's breast. Everything slipped out of focus and the day hung askew. She slid off the float and sank down below the pool's surface, needing a moment of absolute privacy. She squeezed the thing she held in her fist, trying to make it invisible, knowing that she couldn't release it to float again in the glittering sunlight. She would have to think of what to do.

Meanwhile, someone sat beside the pool, amputated, incomplete, probably playing cards, perhaps with a glass in her hand, perhaps not even aware of her bizarre loss, this second one such a thin echo of the first.

Or perhaps, just possibly, oh so much more likely, someone sat with beating heart, sick with embarrassment and despair, wondering where oh where, knowing that she must survive this as she had survived the other horrors was it cancer new breasts for old she could cry swinging along beside the pool with her wares is it a left or a right and why not people lose teeth and eyes and legs and fingers and the sun also rises and the bombs fall and they will patch themselves as best they can and leave their scattered members in the tall grass as they play canasta through the long hot summer.

She emerged, dripping, at the far, the un-peopled end of the pool, casting about for a clue, a sign. There was none. What to do? She shivered, wanting a towel, wanting a cigarette, wanting a drink, unable to take a step. Her father had concluded his descent and, on his way to join his guests, paused for a word with her.

"I ought to get a government subsidy," he said. "I'm running a Goddamn state park."

She tried to smile.

"You all right?" He peered at her, frowning. "Pull yourself together, kid."

Pull yourself together indeed, she thought, as he marched on. How literal he was, if he only knew. He'd been telling her the same thing every day since it had begun. Her mother, too, with her power of positive thinking, her will power. But what could any of them know about her treacherous, scattered body and the Thing, the rot was it? in her head, the Thing that was there waiting, waiting, fooling even the foolish doctors with their foolish tests that proved nothing.

"My poor child, you're shivering," Alex said gently, wrapping a towel around her. She had watched his approach blindly, and was startled by his touch. "Are you cold? On such a lovely warm day?"

She hugged the towel around her. Beneath it, what she held was safe, hidden.

"Have you got a cigarette?" she asked. She could circle the perimeter of the pool, staring at chests, what an idea! Alex put a cigarette between her lips and held a lighted match to it. Gratefully, she drew breath, pulling fire from his hand, drawing his substance, his strength. How intimate. She raised her eyes to meet his and saw in his look that he knew what she was thinking but of course that wasn't possible, people can't know each other that well without first knowing each other much better.

"Come, my love," he said, circling her arm with his large strong hand. "We'll warm you up with a walk. I need to talk to you."

Firmly, he guided her past the bath houses and beyond to a trail that led into the woods. She was glad to go; an idea would come to her as they walked. She could simply leave it in the women's bath house. No, then everyone would see it; whoever had lost it might not want to be exposed. Should she give it to her mother and be done with it? Her mother might know whose it was.

"You look so troubled, my dear," Alex said softly. "Why won't you let me help you?"

The concern in his voice touched off tears of self pity. She blinked them back. "How could you help me!" she said irritably.

He stopped and turned her so that she faced him. "I love you," he said simply.

She sighed, tempted. She didn't trust it, but how nice it was to be loved. Could the right kind of love transform her, cure her? Did she believe in fairy tales?

"Loving isn't enough," she said, turning away. The path was slippery with pine needles. She walked a few steps past him and sat upon a rock. A shaft of sunlight, glancing through the trees, warmed her cheek. "I'm loved now."

"Yes," he said, sitting on the ground at her feet. "But not, I think, in a way that is right for you."

They were going to have one of their "conversations." He was so adept at making her feel like a woman. Without ever having made love. They had never even kissed.

"I could teach you who you are," he said, and inexplicably she thought of Jake, feeling the ache of loss. "I could help you become what you're so afraid to be. What you must, what you will finally become." She had no idea what he meant, but his voice with its careful English was low and softly pitched and, aware that he was being seductive, she felt quite safe.

"All right," she said.

"All right what?"

"All right yes."

She had resisted him for so many months that she had come to believe his pursuit was a polite gesture, a formality he thought was expected of him, almost a tic, perhaps common to Viennese men, but his face came alive with happiness. He leaned forward and kissed her gently, chastely, cupping her face in his hands. She kept forgetting that he was a dozen years further removed from childhood than she or or Herbie. Beneath the restraint of his kiss, she sensed his waiting passion, and was aroused by it.

"Do you mean it?" he said, his hand sliding from her cheek to her throat, his fingers resting there softly as though he wanted not only to hear but to feel her answer. "Really, do you mean it?"

"Yes."

He smiled, reaching beneath the towel for her hand. "When? Will you meet me in town tomorrow? Monday?"

"Oh Christ," she said, "are we going to have to arrange it?"

"Naturally." He laughed. "Did you want it to be here and now?" Of course she did; she couldn't think a whole day ahead. "Do you want someone to trip over us coupling under the trees? Solly Shapiro, for instance? What have you got in your hand?"

She drew her hand out slowly from beneath the towel and unclenched it, watching the thing spring into shape before his puzzled face.

"What on earth is it?"

"It's a rubber breast."

He laughed uncertainly. "One of those, what they call . . . falsies?"

"No. See how it's shaped. It was made to match. To match the other one." She caught her breath. "I found it. It was floating in the pool. On top of the pool. In the sunlight."

She was crying. He snatched it from her hand and threw it over her head into the woods while she rose, crying, "Don't, oh don't!" her body arching in the direction he had thrown it, wanting to fly after it. His fingers wound tightly around her wrist, pinning her back onto her rock.

"Nonsense," he said. "Whoever was so careless deserves to lose it." His grip softened. "My poor darling, you cannot be responsible for the whole world. It is enough, to begin with, if you learn to be responsible for yourself."

"Please," she said, hating him. "Don't be so bloody pompous."

He pressed her hand and smiled. "I'm sorry. It's because you're in so many ways still such a child. Why does it take American women such a long time to become women?"

"Are we different from European women? I mean, if there hadn't been the war? Hitler?"

"Yes. Now, tell me when. Which day this week?"

"Which day?"

"Which day you will meet me."

"Wednesday," she said. The rock had begun to grow hard beneath her, and the damp bathing suit, drying against her skin, made her itch.

"Good," he said, mysteriously amused. "But tell me, please, why did you choose Wednesday?"

"Is there something wrong with Wednesday? I'm going to be in town on Wednesday."

She caught a glimmer of pain on his face. Slowly, he released her hand. What now, she wondered, waiting.

"So. You are coming to town on Wednesday. May I ask why?"

"I have an appointment with the dentist at ten in the morning."

He sighed, passing a hand across his brow. The pulse in his temple throbbed steadily on. For a moment he had been real, but he was beginning to fade.

"So, then," he said, "You are coming to town on Wednesday to see the dentist. And when you have finished with the dentist you will come to see me?"

"For a brief insane moment that was my thought," she said, beginning to be bored. "Why does that make you so unhappy?"

He groaned. "If you cannot see it for yourself, I don't see how I can explain it."

"If I could see it, you wouldn't need to explain it," she said, thinking: my savior! Only a minute earlier, this man was going to save her. She laughed. "Oh, Alex, I've hurt your feelings!"

"Does that amuse you?" It was clear that if she had hurt him before, she was hurting him even more now. "Am I not supposed to have feelings?"

She touched his hand. "Of course I understand. You don't want me to 'fit you in.' You want me to fly to you magically, marvelously, passionately, inconveniently. But don't you see? If I could do that, if I could consider your deepest feelings, if I could love you . . . " But now the hour, staring up at her from the vacuous face on his wrist, drove everything from her mind but guilt.

"Damn!" she said, getting up off her rock, coming unstuck like a long, tired kiss. "It's way past time for Nicky's bath."

He followed half a step behind as she strode along, cursing.

"Shit, shit shit!" she muttered. "Organs and glands check out and lo! another mother. A mother! Anyone. Even an idiot like me."

"Why did you marry him, Annie?"

"Before you're even sure you're a woman, let alone a person there you are, for God's sake, a mother!"

"Why did you marry Herbie, Ann? He's all wrong for you."

"Why, why, why!" Why had she married Herbie? Why was she a mother? Why had she nearly fallen into this man's arms? Why did she wake in the night with her head full of death? Why anything?

Still, she considered his question. "Did you ever watch what happens on people's faces when they look at someone who is unusually good looking?" she said. "I mean, it always happens."

"What happens?"

They were rounding the bath houses from where she saw that the mob around the pool had thinned.

"It's a small thing, but nice," she said. She was talking about Herbie. "And invariable. First a sort of surprise, a small lifting of the eyebrows. And then this little melting thing. Pleasure, interest, a kind of acquiescence." Her voice turned bitter. "Most people have to work for that, but *they* don't have to do anything; it comes with the package. They probably don't even know about it."

The playpen was empty. Herbie was gone, too. Only the card players remained.

"Herbie took him," her mother said without looking up, cigarette smoke curling from her nostrils. She snapped a card down on the table. "They went up five minutes ago."

"I'm going to get dressed," Alex said, walking off to the bath house. "I'll see you up at the house."

She started for the hillside in pursuit of Herbie and Nicky. Guilt lay on her stomach like an undigested meal. She was doing great, just great, a huge success. Her future was spread out before her, a shining panorama of all the things she was going to bring off: wifehood, motherhood, personhood. Plus *poetry*!

When she reached the bottom step, she was arrested by a movement in a clump of evergreens between her and the pool. Startled, she turned, peering into the bushes. Someone was in there lurching, staggering about in some kind of crazy dance. The hemlocks swayed and bent.

"Who is it?" she called, frightened.

"Sme," the figure said, half emerging, pale and disheveled. It was the countess, very drunk. "Sjus lil ole me looking for m'lil ole kitty." She staggered out of the brush to confront Ann with her tense pale face, the flat glare of her dead green eyes.

"You happen to see it?" she said, then shook her head despondently. She turned away and went on with her search. She held one hand before her, thumb and forefinger rubbing against each other, her voice low and persuasive, calling, "Psss, psss, here kitty, kitty, kitty."

"A cat?" Ann said stupidly. "Kitty?" Then, knowing, her heart plummeted. "Oh my God," she said, and grabbed the countess's arm. She pulled her over to the step. "Listen, Tanya, sit down here," she said. "Sit down on this step, okay?"

"Okay," the countess said, sitting. "Why?"

"I know where it is. I'm going to go and get it now, you hear?"

"You know where she is?" She yawned hugely.

"Yes. Wait right here. You won't move? Countess? Your highness?"

"Wait right here no moving absolooly."

Ann turned and ran, impelled by a terrible urgency. She ran past the bath houses and up the trail, back into the woods. The sun had dipped behind the trees and the woods were darkening. She raced past the rock, still damp from her visit, and into the thick growth. She must find it. She would find it. She felt chilled and lonely. Her chest was tight with its dreadful ache. Night was coming and in the night she died. Her eyes streamed tears.

Methodically, systematically, she began to search.

TEN: (then)

"Conversion hysteria," Dr Kantfogel said during their thirteenth hour as analyst and analysand. Since he so rarely told Ann anything except by way of a question, she said, just to make sure, "Are you asking or telling?"

"You asked, I'm telling."

True, she had been asking for weeks what is it? what is it? what is it? After the months of seeing specialists who told her only what "it" was not, of giving away so many specimens and samples that it was hard to believe there could be anything left of the original, she felt like a ghost. Not only were there loss of balance, vertigo, and the peculiar sounds in her head, but colitis, and, most recently, a hideous rash that began innocuously beneath her wedding ring, causing her to stop wearing it, though the rash had gone on anyway to spread and deepen so that both hands were painfully useless, disgustingly ruined. "Tuesday I went from the eye man to the skin man," she told Dr. Kantfogel. "The eye man put drops in my eyes so that, added to my woes, for two hours I was practically blind. I took a taxi to the dermatologist and groped my way into his office. There was no one in the waiting room, I could see that much, or at least I sensed it, and almost at once a white blur opened a door and said come in, and I stumbled in the direction of his voice. I've just come from the eye doctor, I said, and he put those rotten drops in my eyes, and I'm still blind. He took my arm and led me to a chair, then swam behind his desk and began to ask the questions doctors ask, mostly so they'll know where to send the bill. I could tell from his voice that he was young. Okay, Ann, he said when he'd gotten all the information he needed, now let's talk about me. Why, what seems to be your problem, I asked. Loneliness, he said, loneliness and disappointment. Anti-climax. Am I your very first patient? I asked. No but you're my last of the day. Well, you haven't cured me yet, I said, to give him something to look forward to. You haven't even looked at these disgusting hands. I've looked at them, he said, it's eczema, do you use bleach? Ammonia? What do you mean, why would I use them? Do you clean with them around the house? No, I hardly lift a finger, I said, except Nicky's urine smells like ammonia and I change his diapers, could it be that? I doubt it, who knows, it's probably psychological. You're inspiring me with confidence, I said. Yeah, he said, I don't know why I ever went into skin; maybe because I don't get to see much blood. Do you faint at the sight of blood? I asked. No, but I saw so much of it in Spain, enough to last a lifetime. The bullfights? I asked. No, I was in the Abraham Lincoln Brigade, he said, I was the second youngest in the brigade. As soon as he said this I knew he'd been dying to tell it to me from the beginning, not only to impress me, but to reassure himself. No kidding, I said, and I was impressed, you must be passionately political. I am, he said. Is that why all else is anti-climax? I asked, like a great athlete who's washed up at twenty-nine? My life is in ruins, he said. I no longer love my wife if I ever did, I married too young, and my son has asthma and we're going to have to move to some shitty desert, Arizona or New Mexico. It's beautiful in Arizona and New Mexico, I said, though I've never been to either, and deserts are awe-inspiring, like oceans. What kind of life is that for a man like me, he said. What kind of man is that, I asked. A man who needs to be in the thick of things, an activist with an inquiring mind, a political man as well as a scientist, to say nothing of a humanist, in short, a man of broad interests and wide learning with terrific energy. A vital man. A lovable man. By this time he was holding me in his arms, don't ask me how, and kissing me. It was nice but I pushed him away and said why are you kissing me, a total stranger, I can't even see you. The important thing, he said, is that I can see you, let's make love. Not on our first date, I said, though I could tell I'd like it if we did make love. Maybe because of the blurred vision, nothing seemed real. Don't be stuffy, he said, there's not enough time in life for stuffiness. You're right, I said, but it's late and I have to go home and nurse the baby. A lie. I was halfway out the door when I remembered why I'd come. What about my hands, I asked. What hands, he said. Oh! here's some salve, rub it on twice a day, it won't do much good. Thanks, I said, and don't bother to send a bill."

She lit a cigarette and waited for Dr. Kantfogel to say something. It was his turn. Nothing.

"That's the end," she told him.

"You tell a nice anecdote," he said, yawning. "If that's the way you want to spend your money."

"What do you mean?" she cried, stung. "Don't you think that's important? What am I supposed to talk about? I don't even know what I have."

"Conversion hysteria."

"What?"

"That's what you have. Among other things."

- 100 -

"Conversion hysteria?"

"It's a label. You want one, there it is."

"Explain it."

"It's obvious. You explain it."

"Who's hysterical? I'm really quite calm. Of course, when I believe that death is imminent, I get scared. Anyone would. But I don't think I get hysterical."

"Hysteria isn't only on the surface, laughing and screaming. You've been to every kind of doctor there is. You've had every test known to medical science. And what? Nothing."

"Are you trying to tell me I'm imagining it? Are you saying that when I have colitis that isn't real shit? Look at these hands, for God's sake, that's not real?"

She was off the couch, her hands thrust under the doctor's nose. "Tell the truth, when have you seen a worse looking pair of hands?"

"It's real, it's real. I'm not saying you aren't suffering. Now get back on the couch. You still have twelve minutes."

Two dollars a minute. She lay back down on the couch.

"You mean," she said slowly, struggling, "that I convert my hysteria, which I don't even think I have, into all these physical things?"

"You're getting warm. Look at your hands. What do they look like?"

"Ghastly." There were fissures so deep you could almost see bone, and where there was skin it was scaling and gray. "It looks like . . . decay." She choked on the word. "My hands are rotting. Dead and rotting. Like my brain."

"Now we're getting somewhere."

"They're revolting," she said, and thought about what she had said. "Revolting? But against what?"

She could tell from the quality of the silence behind her that Dr. Kantfogel was beaming, that she had made him happy. "Are you saying that I've gone to all this trouble to make a metaphor?" she asked, her heart beginning to thump with fear. "But don't you see, if I can do this without willing it, I could also kill myself!"

"You won't go that far," he said confidently.

"How do you know?"

"You don't want to die."

"I don't? Then why am I doing all *this*? I don't want this suffering, either."

"You don't do it deliberately . . . consciously."

"My subconscious has all that power over me?"

"It is also you, your subconscious. More than you know."

"It's trying to tell me something?"

"Both tell and keep you from knowing."

"Why would it want to do that? Why doesn't it just come right out with it?" Dreams. The stories her dreams told her were true stories disguised, messages from the underground. In code.

She looked at her hands. "Symbols? Distractions? Because reality is too frightening?"

"Bravo."

It was the new internist who had finally said, "No, it's not a brain tumor or cancer or nicotine poisoning. Go on and smoke. Ann, you're having a nervous breakdown." He said it gently, smiling benevolently, and jotted a name and phone number on a slip of paper and gave it to her. "Go see him. He's a good man."

What a relief! A nervous breakdown. Thank God! She was no longer alone, grappling terror in the dark. Her nervous breakdown had brought her and this dandy little doctor together, her Dr. Kantfogel. Twice her age, half her height, her shrunken shrink, and she was already madly in love with him. Crazy about. Crazy, nuts, insane about. She was unable to find an idiom, a slangwich, for "in love" that didn't fall within the precincts of her beloved's field.

The doctor had explained to her that her love for him was part of the process, called transference, another label, but an encouraging sign. It was a useful tool. It meant that maybe they would be able to make some progress. By this time, she had done a little reading on the subject, enough to impress her, not quite enough to convince her.

"What is love ever about?" she asked. "Doesn't there always have to be some illusion? And trust? So that one can surrender a power to the other?"

"That is not what love is about."

"What is it about? You're the one person with the power to give me back my so-called self. Maybe. Even if I do have to pay you. Why shouldn't that make me love you?"

"We're not here to make definitions for love. When you are well and can bring your emotions into some kind of harmony and balance with your intelligence, as well as vice versa, then we will talk about what is love. Meanwhile, there is reality."

"Aren't my feelings real?"

"They may be real but they are inappropriate. Describe me."

She was lying, as always, on the leather couch and he, classically, sat behind her, his notebook in his lap.

"No, don't turn around. Close your eyes and describe me."

"Ah, you think I don't see you," she said, closing her eyes. "You Russian Jew. It's true you're not my type, or what I ever thought of as my type. Fortyish, five foot five, maybe 150 pounds. A hawk in peacock's feathers. Strong jaw, chin, mouth. Thin graying hair, probably blonde once. Your eyes behind those horn-rimmed glasses are pale blue but sharp, your nose is beaky, you're always carefully shaved, cologned, beautifully groomed, expensively dressed. One can see the soft, fine texture, the feel of everything you wear. You are a sensualist and there is so much self-love in you that sometimes it makes you chuckle; you *kvell*. Your torso is strong, your hands expressive, your feet in their glove-soft Italian shoes . . . "

"English."

". . . are small. Everything you could, can, do inside and out, you have done, even down to that fancy malachite and silver cane, to compensate for your withered, crippled legs and your stunted growth. Was it polio?"

"Yes."

"How old were you?"

"A baby. Not yet a year."

"And you grew up enraged."

"Cursing God every morning, shaking my fist at the heavens, shouting, 'God damn you, God,' because my first thought every day was remembering, because to get out of bed I had to put on the braces first. I wanted to spring up, fly, but the heaviness . . . Like chains . . . " He caught himself and sighed, embarrassed. "What are we doing now? Wasting your money again. All right, congratulations, so you see me. Who else do you see?"

"Herbie tells lies," she said, biting a cuticle.

"How do you mean?"

"Crazy things. Little things. I'm beginning to think he does it all the time."

"For instance."

"He calls me from the office at least once a day, just to chat, to see how I am. Yesterday, when he called he told me he'd heard on the radio that they'd found a cure for cancer. Naturally, I was excited and the rest of the day I kept turning on the radio for the news. Nothing. Nothing in the paper last night or this morning. Nothing about a new drug, even, or a new theory. Nothing at all, not one word about cancer, probably the only day of completely cancer-free news in my lifetime, even on the obituary page."

"Did you question him?"

"Of course."

Lying in the tub, parboiled, the steam rising to clear her sinuses and to fog the medicine-chest mirror, she was soaping the concavity between her hipbones where some day, when eating was again an adventure and a delight, she would grow a respectable, perhaps too respectable, stomach.

"I wish you'd put on a little weight," Herbie said. "You're losing your sex appeal."

It was a long, deep generous tub, one she fit in without having to fold herself into segments. More important, it was hers, hers and Herbie's.

"Stick to the subject," she said. He was sitting on the closed toilet seat, rewiring a lamp, keeping her company.

"Shit, this knife is no damn good," he said. "I need a wirestripper. What was the subject?"

How domestic they were, at last making their own nest in this spacious, bright new apartment, two bedrooms and two baths and, from one of the bedroom windows, between two identical cubes of prisonbrick buildings, a six-inch view of the East River, if you angled your head properly. The apartment still had the fresh damp smell of its construction and all day it reverberated with rattling and pounding, the completing of the complex's last few buildings. Since it was the first major postwar residential construction, the management had been swamped with supplicants and there were already long waiting lists when Herbie flew to the rental office straight from seeing Dr. Kantfogel, who enjoined him to "get her out of there, out of her parents' castle, I don't care how gorgeous it is, and into your own place. That's step number one." Everyone had said it was already impossible to get an apartment there, but it had taken Herbie exactly three days to sign the lease and get the key.

"I didn't bribe him," Herbie insisted. "I charmed him." "Him" was the young man in the rental office who interviewed Herbie. "Only fourteen more weeks to Christmas, I reminded him over lunch at the Plaza. 'Is there anything in particular you'd like, or should I just go ahead and order the Jaguar?'"

Whatever he'd done, she was thankful. She loved the apartment. They were still furnishing it, and she often touched a wall, the bathroom tile, a kitchen cabinet, ran her hand down the refrigerator door, with a sensual thrill of possession: this is mine, and this is mine, and this; furthermore, virginal, it had never been anyone else's, though of course it all belonged to their megacorporate landlord. The intensity of her pleasure surprised her into recognition of the extent of her deprivation. All her homes had been her father's and she had always been suffered not to share them, but to intrude on them. When, as a child, she damaged or broke anything, the house resounded with her father's rage. She had committed an unforgivable sin against his money. ("I work like a dog to have a decent home and all you know is to wreck it.") Not that she had been any more destructive than most children, but she learned early to be careful, to tread lightly. Even while they were living at Sleepy Hollow Acres, her father constantly lost his temper over phone bills, heating bills, food bills, making Ann feel, even in the lap of all that luxury and ostentation, like a guilty child. Her father's eyes would grow small and mean and his mouth ugly and wide, his anger bellowing forth from it. As though a button had been pressed, she would respond as she must have done from infancy, with fear, with anger, with hatred, with helplessness. Her childhood.

Yet how furious her father was with them now for leaving. They had deprived him of a rationale for such a huge place, far too grand for just the two of them. Enraged, he had put it on the market.

With Dr. Kantfogel, she had recognized that the onset of her nightly panic coincided with the sun's setting. During the years of her growing up, home had seemed pleasant and serene during the day, but as night and the hour of her father's homecoming approached, everyone grew tense, particularly Ann's mother, and Ann would feel a tightening in her own stomach. The suspense of waiting to see what his mood would be when he came through the door, and mostly it was foul, the barometer of what his own day had seemed like to him, charged the air with a sense of impending invasion and menace.

"I guess the only way I could leave home was by marrying," she told Dr. Kantfogel. By the time she was grown, she lacked the confidence, the self-esteem, the courage, to leave in any other way. She had chosen Herbie because he was so clearly her father's opposite. He was affectionate, easygoing, loving, and so far, in the three years of their marriage, had never lost his temper. She had never actually seen him angry, nor even indignant. She had almost no idea what he really thought or felt about anything, not that she hadn't asked. She was asking now.

"The subject," he said, distractedly, his lips pursed in concentration as he threaded a split wire around a screw. "Your sexiness, wasn't it? There's nothing on you to grab hold of anymore."

"You're impossible, Herbie," she said. "If Jay Howland is a party member, as Doris says, and is infiltrating our chapter, why does it matter? He's our most effective member." They had joined the newly formed chapter of the American Labor Party, its membership comprised of neighbors, all new to the community and surprisingly homogenous, young parents, mostly, and all of them white. It was rectifying this last that was their first order of business. "He's the most fearless and outspoken of us all, and the most practical." Jay had organized the petitions, the press releases, the picket line.

"Yeah," Herbie said, "I don't see any way he could be a threat."

She had cued him and he was giving back her own answer. As always. He had no objections to thinking whatever he thought she wanted him to think. He couldn't care less. Having chosen him, albeit unconsciously, because he was so unlike her father, was she so irritated with him now because he wasn't enough like her father, or because she had gone too far and chosen some stupid other extreme? Had she chosen? Please, Herbie, think, feel, believe. Something. Anything.

"The word is that if they take over the A.L.P. and enough other organizations, eventually they'll take over the country. And the world."

"Nonsense."

"And when they do, your business will be among the first to go. Not such a bad thing, either."

"What have you got against my business? It pays the rent on this swell place you're so happy to be in."

"It doesn't *do* anything."

"It does so. It's a service business."

"It's unnecessary. It doesn't produce or distribute or uplift or entertain or inform or advance or discover or repair or conserve."

"It's a sales tool."

"It's the ultimate wart on the Body Capitalism."

"How poetic! It's not a wart. I won't have you saying that Becker, O'Toole and Shimkin is a wart. I think you're more of a threat to this nation than Jay."

"Herbie, about that cancer thing."

"Which cancer thing?"

"That you heard on the radio yesterday."

"Oh, yeah."

"Did you really hear it?"

"Isn't it strange? Just that and then not another word?"

He was looking at her with that odd, glazed, almost vulnerable look, as though he had pulled a thin shade over his eyes to shield them against the glare of some too bright danger. Was she the danger? Sometimes, when he looked at her with love, that same thing was in his eyes. Was he afraid of her? Did he really hate her?

"He finally conceded," she told Kantfogel, "that maybe he'd misunderstood, that he was only half listening."

"How could he misunderstand such a thing? Is he a little deaf?"

"No. But why would he make it up?"

"How did it make you feel?"

"Happy, naturally." Her maternal grandfather had died in his early fifties of stomach cancer, leaving a legacy of nervous stomachs lined up, waiting to be next. "Who wouldn't rejoice at news like that?"

"So he told you this, made it up, to make you happy?"

"A gift to me? But how stupid," she said, knowing at once that it was true, that this was one of Herbie's I love you's. "He had to know I'd find out it wasn't true and be disappointed and angry. It's so much worse than if he hadn't said anything."

It would take her a while longer to learn that this wasn't one of Herbie's ways of saying I love you. He was saying love me. He said it to everyone.

ELEVEN: (Now)

My mother and I are having lunch in the golf club's dining room. Our table, next to a curved glass wall, overlooks an avenue of palms that divides the seventeenth and eighteenth holes. The view includes some colorful ducks, one of them a mother, trailed, like an inconclusive sentence meandering off into dots, by her perky file of downy young. In this over-developed part of Florida, so few places have been left to nature that the oases of golf courses have come to be preserves. The ducks live happily on the seventeenth hole, a water hole, taking frequent strolls along the fairway, as they are doing now, unruffled by the aged athletes puttering by in their electric carts, driving to meet the balls they've sent on ahead.

At the first hole, a mocking bird sounded its derisive cry from a treetop just as my mother teed off, her usual drive, straight and true and about twenty yards long. I could have thrown it farther. My mother cocked an eye at the bird and said, "Nothing personal, I hope." She was happier than she'd been since my arrival.

We played nine holes. My mother, who never really learned to drive an automobile, probably because my father was never able to sit back and trust her, handled the golf cart like a jockey, with skill and pleasure. She's been playing golf four or five times a week since they moved south, claiming that golf is what keeps her young. Yet golf as it's played here bears little resemblance to the sport as I've known it, the brisk walk across hilly fairways. This course, like most of Florida, is flat, and the only exercise involved consists of climbing in and out of the cart to take whacks at the ball.

"At my age it's enough exercise," my mother says. "It gets me out in the air and away from your father."

Angie would love it, I think, remembering the one hilarious day we played golf together. Though not an athlete, Angie is extraordinarily physical, moving always with that unselfconsciousness of people who have never been made to feel that they are taking up too much room, who are so much at one with their bodies that even when they fall down (drunk) they do it with aplomb. She's a good swimmer and knows all about fishing; she has that silent, mysterious instinct for where her fish would be, what it's looking for, how to lure it and take it, a Zen transport. I loved to watch her stillness, her frowning concentration, the small, questioning movements of her hands, and then their swift, sure competence when they were challenged by her prey. Limber, catlike, lithe, she's incapable of making a movement that isn't graceful and stylish, her light and airy walk, the way she can spring to her feet in one easy motion from the lotus position on the floor, dancing to that sad, beautiful Mahler waltz from Des Knaben Wunderhorn that she played over and over, dancing that magical night of the party when we were all so happy, dancing with Duncan? Philip? waltzing in that gossamer black gown that made her skin look so golden, her head high and slightly tilted to one side, her eyes shining, her body fluid and sure, she and the waltz inextricably joined, parts of an organic whole. I've never been able to hear that waltz again without feeling an almost unbearable sense of loss. Sometimes I play it just to torture myself.

The waitress brings menus, fills the water glasses.

"The shrimp salad is good here," my mother says. We both order it. It's an attractive dining room. The tables are round and generous, covered with bright orange cloths, and the room, too, is round, bright, and spacious, with tables on two levels.

"I was here for a bridge luncheon last week," my mother says. "A benefit. Some woman dropped dead."

"Here?"

"A woman named Anna Kretchmer, Kratzmore, something like that, Tina knows her, I only knew her slightly. On her way in to the luncheon."

"Here in the dining room?"

She points to a spot in the path alongside a small service bar where patrons entering the dining room pass on their way to the tables.

"They called the rescue squad. It was too late."

"But before the rescue squad came? The women were still coming in? Did they just come in and walk around her? Tell me."

"What did you want them to do, walk over her?"

"Mother! Didn't they stop them at the door?"

"I guess nobody thought of it. People are taken by surprise. They did cover her."

"They covered her? With what?"

"A tablecloth."

"One of these? These orange ones?"

"That's all they have here," she says, defensively. "They don't have black table cloths."

"And the women went on with their luncheon? And then played bridge?"

"What should they have done, gone home? If everyone went home every time someone dies here, they could close up the whole state."

"You actually sat here eating shrimp salad . . ."

"Chicken salad. It was Wednesday."

". . . while that poor woman lay newly dead under an orange tablecloth?"

"Better newly. She was gone by the time we started lunch. The whole thing was only about ten minutes. Oh God, Ann, I'm sorry I ever mentioned it." She takes a long pull on her cigarette and the smoke dances out of her mouth. "Naturally we were affected. Everyone spoke in hushed voices."

In spite of myself, I laugh. "Poor Anna Kretchmer or Kratzmore," I say, "ending the long serious business of her life, her *life*, like that."

"My daughter, the poet. So sensitive."

TWELVE: (then)

"What a dandy little contraption you are," she told Dr. Kantfogel. "What a nifty trick to sell me your ears."

She was warming up. It wasn't easy to come in out of the everyday world, throw yourself onto a couch, and come up with plums of insight. "Although if I paid you for the time you actually listened, I'd be entitled to a discount." What wouldn't she give to have a tape of his thoughts while she lay there, toiling down memory lane, mumbojumboing her way through the maze of psychosoma that had her paralyzed and pinned to his cleverly cracked leather couch, his not bad prints and etchings blurring in and out of her memories of trauma.

"If you paid me for the time you actually said something, you'd save yourself a lot of money."

"Money. Sex and money."

"Never underestimate the importance of money." It wasn't the first time he'd said it. "It wouldn't surprise me if it's an even more potent force than sex."

"Force for what?"

"Motivating."

"Good and evil, what ever became of those?" she asked. "Love and honor?"

Yawn, yawn, yawn.

"The simple virtues? The eternal verities?"

"Glib," he said. "You think your glibness is a defense, but it's your nemesis, a trap you fall into."

Stung, she saw how he could be right. She had always been glib; there had always been words.

"I was the only one in my class who didn't have a middle name," she said, infuriated. "What a shocking discovery that was. I went home in a rage and screamed at my mother for her laziness. 'You didn't even think enough of me to bother with a middle name,' I accused her. 'And when it came to a first name all you could manage was three lousy little letters, nothing more than a slightly elongated article. I'm surprised you didn't name me The.' She said she would have if she had known how I was going to turn out. 'I haven't turned out yet,' I said, 'I'm just beginning to turn out.'"

"Stop!"

"Stop?"

"Tell me how you felt when you first started to menstruate. Can you remember?"

It was her turn to yawn. Who wanted to talk about that? But thanks to his shove, they had now traversed the tunnel-opening into one of their long black silences. She peered into the gloom for a glimmer of light. How to proceed? There were so many levels. Layers and layers. Start with the physical.

"I thought it was degrading and badly planned," she said. "People can cope with excreta that can be controlled, dumped at will in specific places. One of our earliest traumas is being persuaded to do that, and acquiring a healthy revulsion at the idea of soiling ourselves. But imagine if the planning in that department had been as careless as that for menstruation. Imagine, for instance, four or five days of shit dribbling from your nostrils."

The doctor groaned.

"What I'm trying to say is: if that's the way our plumbing was arranged, we'd have to find some way of dealing with it. Tubes running up our nostrils, attached, perhaps, to little colostomy backpacks. Okay, the menstrual arrangement isn't quite that bad. At least the orifice involved is otherwise meant to be used merely for sexual pleasure and begetting, and most of the time it's concealed."

"Your time is cheap, but why must you waste mine?"

"I'm trying to explain why I felt so affronted, so indignant. It seemed to me that if nature was going to program women for all that bleeding, it ought to have provided some natural, built-in way of disposing of it. It seemed insane that industries should have sprung up to profit from blood blotting."

"Other places, other times, they'd have sent you out of the clearing into the woods to squat over a hole for five days."

"I count my blessings. Now. But then I was an ignorant child of thirteen whose body had always been a swift and marvelous vehicle, the Ferrari of my soul, and overnight had become a . . . a *patient*, requiring peculiar ministrations. Suddenly, I was Florence Nightingale running with bandages to my own vagina."

"Cunt. Say cunt."

She winced. He was always trying to get her to use words like that, words she didn't even think. "I don't think that way. I never have. Honestly. So I was mad at God, or Whoever. There seemed to be so much waste in nature. Being a woman meant that for the next forty years of my life I was going to have to buy boxes of what amounted to little toilets. In sizes. It was ignominious. Forests would be denuded, mills would grind, women in factories would grow old folding, packing. And I haven't even begun to mention the discomfort, the headaches, cramps, moodiness, embarrassment."

"Embarrassment?" he asked hopefully.

She glanced at her watch. Some hours were endless. She closed her eyes so that she could be thirteen, brooding on bleeding, resentful that she must carry around this wound, yet cheered on by her peers, her mother, her aunts, her grandmother. She had turned a corner. She was one of them. She was, after all, despite so much evidence to the contrary, normal. With no effort on her part, she had achieved something.

Then the understanding came, that gut knowledge of what she had been suspecting. Propagation was what it was all about. ALL. Keeping things going. The rest was subsidiary, put there to make you feel important, dignified, meaningful, so that you wouldn't just let the race die out. Things like freedom and liberty and mysticism and justice and art and kindness. And love and passion and blah blah blah. But the main thing, the meaning of it all, was reproduction. And the spur, the carrot, was sex!

Sex, therefore, must be okay, maybe more than okay. She had read enough to know that people were obsessed with sex. They loved it, feared it, embraced it, shunned it, were ruined or uplifted by it, made a living at it or a hobby of it, couldn't get enough of it, got too much of it and grew jaded, were inspired by it or ashamed of it, were successful at it or never quite got the hang of it, joked about it, flaunted it, whispered and blushed, committed it sinfully or joyously. Doing it could give you diseases or clear up your complexion, while abstinence made you serene and saintly, or nervous and cranky.

"Glib, glib, glib," the doctor sighed.

"But as brash and opinionated as I was about everything else, I had no idea how I felt about sex. I'd tried out kissing and that was all right, but otherwise I had absolutely no notion . . ."

The doctor tossed in his chair. "Masturbation." he mumbled.

"I never did it."

"Nobody," he said firmly, "never masturbated."

"To this day."

"I hate to call you a liar."

"I'm not lying. When I was four I had gonorrhea and I had to go . . ."

"You had what?"

"Gonorrhea. My mother referred to it as a social disease. How could a disease be social, I wondered, when social was jolly, convivial? Then she said its real name was gonorrhea and that I was not to mention it to the neighbors."

"One minute please, if you don't mind. You've been coming into this office and lying on that couch for, what, eight months? And this is the first time you see fit to mention that when you were four years old you had a venereal disease?"

"I'm trying to explain why I never masturbated. You see, the treatment was awful. For a whole summer I had to go to a doctor three times a week and lie on a table with my legs spread, I think my ankles were strapped, while the doctor did something to my vagina with a flame, I seem to remember, but maybe I've got it wrong. Whatever it was it burned, burned, burned, and I screamed and screamed and thank God it didn't last too long. When it was over, Patrick usually took me to a movie."

She could tell that the doctor was interested. He was thrashing about in his chair.

"So, you see, because there was all that pain and shame and fuss and trauma connected with it, it never occurred to me to seek pleasure there. In later years, what a surprise to find that it was such a happy little place. But back then I touched it only with wash cloths or toilet paper, and only when it was absolutely essential."

"Let's get this straight," the doctor said, his voice strained. "You had gonorrhea when you were four. Three times a week you went to the doctor for painful and frightening treatments. Then Patrick took you to the movies. May I inquire who Patrick was?"

"Calm down, Dr. Kantfogel. He was our chauffeur."

"The chauffeur took you to the doctor for those treatments?" He was practically screaming. "Where the hell was your mother?"

Ann thought about it. "She did take me the first few times. Then I guess it got to be a drag. We couldn't go away that summer on account of me, so she joined a golf club. I guess that's where she was, at the golf club."

"We'll set the issue of your mother aside for the moment. Let me ask you one small question. Who were you fucking?"

"What do you mean, who was I, er, fucking?" she forced herself to say. He thought he was liberating her. He thought she was linguistically repressed. "I wasn't, er, fucking anyone. I was four years old."

"So how did you contract this disease?"

"My mother said I got it from not putting paper on a strange toilet seat. By strange she didn't mean peculiar, she meant alien."

"I am a medical doctor as well as a psychiatrist, as you know, and it has always been my understanding, as well as that of my colleagues, that the only way to get gonorrhea is through direct genital contact. That usually involves what you call 'er fucking'."

"That's crazy. That's certainly something I'd re-member. Besides, as I've told you, I was a virgin when I got married. It was hell breaking down that barrier."

"THERE IS ONLY ONE WAY TO GET GONORRHEA. THINK!"

She was stunned by Kantfogel's news. In movies and books, early childhood events locked away for years are suddenly revealed, explaining everything: the accidental murder of a sibling, a terrible moment of incest, witnessing the primal scene, a glimpse of one's mother as harlot, ROSEBUD. Could she have a buried mystery? Oh, how she hoped so! She closed her eyes and thought.

"It's true that I was in love with Patrick," she said af-ter a while. He was a big Irishman with a large white face and thin pale hair and pale blue eyes. She was in love with him because, unlike her father, unlike most adults, he'd paid attention to her.

"Aha!" said Kantfogel.

"Patrick was carving a huge, intricate, three-masted schooner and whenever I went down to the basement to visit his room and to see how the ship was coming along, we'd have long talks about Ireland and about his sweetheart in County Kerry. Her picture was on the bureau and she looked like a dimwit to me. I was jealous."

He had taught her to draw pictures of sailors and told her long tales about his years at sea.

"I loved the lilt of his voice. I do recall telling him to forget the Old Country and to give up his sweetie and wait for me. I figured I'd be ready in about eleven years. He said he'd think about it. He said that after all the world was a queer place and who could foretell what strange twists of fate the future might hold. But I truly believe that was the extent of the intimacy between us."

"Think."

"I'm thinking as hard as I can. Yes! I remember one really shocking thing."

"Hah!"

"And that was when someone happened to mention that Patrick wasn't Jewish. Until then, I believed that human and Jewish were synonyms. I didn't know what not being Jewish meant so I cried for a long time and then, resigned, I said, all right, tell me who else isn't Jewish, and the list was staggering: Hilda, the black nursemaid who slept in my room until I was three, President Hoover, all the Italian people who worked for my father."

"That's enough!"

"Is my time up?"

"Ann, what are you doing? You're an intelligent, articulate young woman. You could spend years on that couch entertaining me. Is that what you want?"

She began to cry. She tried to stop and found that she couldn't. He held a box of tissues out to her.

"Why am I crying?" she said, blowing her nose.

"Well, why *are* you crying?"

"I keep trying to form scar tissue."

"With your big mouth?"

'"But what is the wound?"

"Well, what is the wound?"

"That I don't know who I am. That I'm not exactly anybody."

"You're somebody."

"I'm not the somebody I'm supposed to be. I don't know which somebody I am."

"Which somebody aren't you?"

"I don't know if I'm the somebody who is Herbie's wife. I'm not sure if I'm even the somebody who is Nicky's mother, who drives with lists to Daitch-Shopwell in the pink and black Dodge station wagon, who keeps track of the toilet paper and dog food and tooth paste and clean socks."

"You will learn to be that somebody. That's why you are here, to learn to accept yourself as a woman, to value yourself, to be happy in your role."

"My *role*?" she said.

Her hour was up.

"It's just possible," he said, when she was at the door, "that the doctor was mistaken."

"What doctor?"

"Twenty years ago it wasn't so easy to diagnose. There are vaginal infections that were sometimes confused with gonorrhea."

She stood with her hand on the doorknob, looking at the doctor, her anger rising. She felt like a circus dog who has just been made to jump through hoops, and who is going to have to go on and on learning new tricks.

"Great," she said. "I'm glad to learn that doctors are fallible."

THIRTEEN: (Now)

My father has functioned admirably in the hospital: sat, walked, taken nourishment, dealt efficiently with his urinary tract and bowels, and maintained a normal body temperature. Most important, his paced heart has been jogging on without faltering. He is about to be discharged.

In my capacity of chauffeur, I'm sitting outside the hospital in his Coupe de Ville thinking of Atropos and her coup de vie. The glare of the Florida sun on the car's creamy hood is blinding, but inside, with the motor gently idling so that ersatz north winds blow through the vents, I wait comfortably, parked near the exit through which he will soon be restored to the world. My mother is in the hospital taking care of the separation procedure. I know how hard it is to be admitted to a hospital, but I can't recall if getting out is any easier. I did it twice, back in that other life, but all I had to do was get dressed and have my sweet swaddled infant handed to me while Herbie did whatever was required deep in the labyrinthine bowels of the institution in which I'd labored.

I watch as my parents come through the automatic glass doors that their weight had caused to slide open. Their weight. Their presence. My parents. My tenuous continuity. Their eyes, finding me in the appointed place, flicker with that tiny triumph of an expectation met. Unexpectedly, tears come; I am inordinately grateful that they are both alive and upright and walking toward me, no matter how slowly, in this moment, in this life, in this place, on this planet. For the moment, I forgive my father everything.

He is bent, his steps tentative. My mother, erect, holds his arm with one hand, his suitcase with the other. They've checked out of many hotels in their joined past, debarked from ships, planes, trains, turned their backs on homes to move to better ones, larger ones, then smaller ones, but I'm pretty sure they've never left a place in this way, with one supporting the other, certainly not with my mother supporting my father. Good chauffeur that I am, I leap from the car to open doors and help my father into the front seat while my mother climbs in back. My father maneuvers slowly, gingerly, grunting.

"Whew!" he says when he's settled. "Am I glad to be out of there. With my feet on the ground, not in it."

I pilot the car out of port and into the sea of traffic. In the rear view mirror I see my mother smiling brightly and nodding. If she were Catholic, my mother would be making the sign of the cross, but instead she wears the smug look of someone who has once again scored a personal victory, weathered yet another crisis, outwitted witless fate.

"This car," my father says fondly, patting the seat beside him, the good leather. The seat is wide enough for four. "You know how old it is?" He's crazy about his old Cadillac, has always given it everything it wanted and needed. The car is as close as a brother. "This car is, Polly, how old is it?"

"It's going on thirteen," she says, surprised that he can have forgotten.

"That's right, it's going to be Bar Mitzvah'd soon," he chuckles.

"Car Mitzvah'd," my mother says, predictably. It's a family failing. "We'll have it catered."

"You know how much mileage you're getting?" I say. "I checked it when I filled it yesterday. Eleven miles to the gallon!"

"Who cares," he says placidly. For some reason, he wants for this car what he doesn't want for anything or anyone else: that it outlive him. "I'm not getting much mileage either."

"Don't treat him like a child," I'd advised my mother that morning in preparation for his homecoming, fascinated by the subtle shift I'd observed during the hospital visits, shifts in the balance between them, my mother's gradual transformation from intimidated concubine, target of his irritation and temper, sinkhole for his rage and frustration, to mother of this aged child who indulges himself at his own expense, who doesn't know, as she does, better. "Don't nag him. If he wants soup for lunch, and he will, he always does, don't tell him he doesn't need it. Let's try to keep him calm, at least for today."

Still, when we're back at the apartment and my father has changed into pajamas and robe, and we're about to sit down to lunch, and he says, "You know what I feel like, Polly? A nice plate of soup. Open a can of split pea," my mother instantly, automatically, reflexively, says, "You don't need it!" her voice stern. Then, reminded by the look on my face, she adds in a reasonable voice, "Split pea is so gassy. How about chicken and stars?"

After lunch, he goes to his bedroom to rest, but reappears almost instantly. "What am I resting for?" he says, going to his desk with its litter of unopened mail. "Who's tired?"

"Max!" my mother says. "That can wait."

"It can't wait. It waited long enough."

"Suppose you had died, God forbid."

"I didn't die," he says, tearing envelopes.

Passing through, on my way to fetch the new Iris Murdoch to take along to the tiny beach, I stop to ask, "Yes, but suppose you had died? Who would know what to do?"

He looks up, pleased at the practical question, pleased that I appear to be "taking an interest."

"Come here, I'll show you," he says. "The way I have everything arranged, anyone could figure it out. Even you." Reluctantly, I abandon Iris Murdoch, and what remains of the afternoon sun, the sea, the brown pelicans feeding today along the shore, their crazy kamikaze plunges for lunch. The remainder of this day, I know at once, is spoken for. I join my father at his desk where, with so much pleasure, he is rummaging for pads, accordion folders, ledgers. He begins to explain his "system."

How neat he is, infinitely neater than his explanations, which are invariably obfuscated when he speaks of money matters, as though he's afraid that if he were comprehensible he would somehow be diminished, that his mastery of the intricacies of business might seem less meaningful if the mysteries were accessible to me or my mother. Does he deliberately put us off by making finance more complex than it is? Is his gibberish calculated? Or are his calculations gibberish? Because he's a neat and orderly man, his twos are twos and his sevens are clearly sevens. Everything is labeled, indexed, filed, cross-filed, cross-indexed, numbered, in apple-pie alphabetical order. There are lists and every item on every list is a record not only of itself but of relatives in other lists, order in his fiscal universe, not merely double entry but ramified-entry, each tiniest monetary whisper resonating in a circular infinity of his creation. Can it all really be necessary? We move from desk drawers to the cabinets beneath the bookshelves, to steel files in the walk-in "office closet," and back again to the desk, until my head begins to spin.

"Aren't you tired?" I mumble. "You just got out of . . ."

"Pay attention. This is important." His pencil stabs a column of figures on a pale green accounting sheet.

"What's this figure?" I ask, pointing to the bottom line.

"This is a list of my holdings," he says. "I'll explain it."

He begins, item by item, to go over it, but my mind is riveted to that bottom line, that total. For years he's been crying about the stock market, which always seems to be falling when he mentions it, about recession, about inflation, about expenses, the cost of living, my mother's extravagance, his limited income since his retirement. He worries about my poverty, how will I manage? It's been years since he's been able to outwit the estate tax by making me the allowable annual gift.

I can see by the date on top of the sheet that this list is current. He spends a lot of his time making lists like this one, to take into account the fluctuations of the market, to keep abreast. This list was made only a day or two before he went into the hospital.

He is explaining about the value of his 53% equity in corporation A and the 60% in corporation B and so on, and these are the bonds (luckily he knew at what moment to get out of stocks and into bonds), and these are the remaining stocks, blue chips only, at his age he isn't interested in equity, only income, but I am only half-listening. I am too stunned.

"Do you mean to tell me," I interrupt, "that after all your crying . . ."

". . . and this is a management fee I pay myself. Naturally it's much less than it should be for my trouble, for the time I put in."

". . . about losses in the market, about how much it's costing you to live . . ."

". . . and this doesn't include what's in Mother's name. That's on another list . . ."

". . . about having to belong to two golf courses, one for golf and one for entertaining . . ."

". . . so when I finish explaining this list, we'll go over Mother's. Now, I want to show you how this figure is broken down in detail in this ledger . . ."

". . . the rent, the jewelry, the trips . . ."

"This is important. I'm trying to explain it so that you'll understand it. What? I'm not supposed to live?"

". . . that you're still worth all that money?"

"The market happens to be up right now. I could be worth a lot less tomorrow."

"I bet you were never worth more."

He thinks about it, then nods. "That's right," he says, unable to conceal his pride. "But with inflation . . ."

"And that's after retiring!"

"If you can call it retiring."

"Will you please tell me WHY I AM SO POOR?"

He stares at me, his face blank.

"Stop shouting at me. What has this got to do with you?"

I'm stopped dead in my tracks. He really means it. What has his money got to do with me?

"Why are you showing all this to me?" I ask, feebly. "Why are you bothering to explain it?"

"Someone should understand it. Your mother certainly can't."

"Not can't. Won't," she corrects from the corner of the room where she's working a Double-Crostic. "I'm not interested."

The blood rises like mercury to his face, indicating the heat of his rage. "See?" he screams. "She's not interested! Only in cigarettes and crossword puzzles and her four o'clock Scotches."

"Calm down," she says.

"All right. Why me?" I persist, trying to make my point. Except in relation to them, I rarely think of myself as "poor." I have a small income from money invested in one of my father's ventures, money from the sale of the house on Red Maple Lane. I give a few paid readings a year and sometimes I teach a course, and I live, even by their standards, carefully. But what is all this money for? It's far more than they can spend, no matter how long they live. Even the income from it must be more than they can spend. Why is he hoarding it?

"Why me?" I repeat. "Why are you explaining all this to me?"

"You're my daughter," he says, although the tone of his voice admits to no real connection. "Listen, I never told you how to live your life," he says. A lie. He has always told me how to live my life. "Maybe what you're doing isn't what you should be doing. Maybe it's a waste of time. There's a lot of things you could have done. You could have written advertising in Herbie's agency if you wanted to write. I didn't tell you to get divorced, either. Herbie was very likable. Whatever else may have been wrong with him, he didn't cheat on you, he didn't drink, and he usually made a living."

There! He has summed it all up, my life. Poetry is a waste of time. I shouldn't have gotten a divorce.

"You're not answering my question," I manage to say, holding my temper.

"Furthermore, you could do yourself a favor and get married again."

"I don't want to get married again," I groan through my teeth.

"So what do you want from me? You want money, get a job. If you can't make a living writing poems maybe it's because you're not good enough, did you ever think of that?"

I know better, but the thought has crossed my mind.

"I know your name," I tell him, from the depths of my demolished ego, "and I know the names of your parents. Period. That's as far back as I can go with the naming of the entire history of Silvers. A distinguished line. But you know what? I just might be the first Silver to leave something behind in this world besides another forgotten Silver."

"A book?" he sneers. "With poems? The world is full of lousy books that, believe me, die even faster than people."

How can I argue with him? The world is full of lousy books.

He pats his chest carefully, mindful of what lies beneath it. "Me, I'm going to leave an estate," he says.

"You're going to leave what?"

"You heard me. An estate."

I slump, defeated. "I can't believe it," I mumble, though I do believe it. When he was growing up early in the century on the lower east side, scrambling for nickels and dimes in his patched knickers, newspaper obituaries often mentioned the size of the estate left by the deceased, especially if he hadn't done anything more serviceable with his life than amass money. "Hyman Mandel, president of Mandel Haberdashers, died last Tuesday, leaving an estate of a little over a million dollars." This made Mr. Mandel a hero in my father's eyes. Obituaries were probably all he read then, before he himself had amassed enough money to invest and could move to the financial pages.

Nonetheless, I persist. "I can't believe it," I repeat. "You're over 80. You're being run by a machine. And that's what you think it's all about? That's the bottom line? An estate?"

Despite his feebleness, he manages to look like Napoleon, like Mussolini, like Picasso. That stubbornness, that arrogance, that absolute authoritarian self-assurance.

"That's right," he says, with pride. "An estate."

FOURTEEN (Then)

She awoke one April morning to spring, and ran to the window to breathe it. How good it smelled! The limbs of the deciduous trees on their third of an acre, oak and beech and one young red maple, were trembling awake with new energy after their long winter's sleep, when they were merely sharp lines etched against the sky, the snow, the dead lawn. She imagined the sap running in them, as she felt the blood quicken in her veins. It was a morning when everything seemed possible.

They had left their city apartment when Jed was born, she reluctantly, hating to part with it, hating to change her life, for this Scarsdale house. It was true that they needed another bedroom, as Herbie insisted, and he had chosen this house and assured her that she would come to love it.

"You've turned me into a suburban housewife and mother," she complained. "I never planned it this way."

Now, looking out at the early spring day, she almost did love it. Then she thought of the demands the garden would soon be making, the chores she should even now be doing, and her euphoria ebbed. Beds to turn, compost to be worked into the soil, stacks of flats filled with bulbs waiting in the basement to be planted. The idea of gardening appealed to her far more than its doing. Ordering nature, shaping it to her vision, was like writing poems or painting pictures. In late May, let the eye find this and this, the air fill with the scent of that. In early June, this corner of the house will be softened thus. In the heat of summer, against those darker greens let these pinks and reds brightly bloom, and when the season turns, when the year's dying lights the flame that will consume it, clothe the garden in the mature dignity of these golds, purples, rusts. She was Merlin creating this shifting panorama on their deeded allotment of earth.

But the doing, like housework, turned to drudgery, leaving in its wake a complex spiral of requirements to keep it all from coming undone. Danger lurked, waiting for her to prepare the soil, plant, nurture, water, weed, stake, prune. Children and pets to be kept off, pests and diseases to be dusted and sprayed against, those natural enemies whose very existence depended on what she planted, so that she felt as if she were creating them, too, the thrips, caterpillars, worms, beetles, aphids, borers, spiders, hoppers, mealybugs, mites, slugs; the virus, fungus, bacteria, rot, botrytis, rust, mildew, scab. Where did it all hover, waiting for her to make her move? It was a wonder that anything grew at all. Yet, if she stopped succoring and tending and left the garden to the anarchy of nature, it would soon turn, mysteriously, not into a desert but a jungle.

She could hear the muffled roar of the vacuum cleaner downstairs. Cory, the au pair from Holland, unsmiling, ruddy, plodding, heavy-footed and reliable, gentle but a little too rigid with Jed, whose precocious humor and mercurial grace she couldn't comprehend.

It was nearly nine. Cory would have made breakfast for Nick and Herbie and they would be gone, Nick on his bike and Herbie in his latest extravagance, a bright little red convertible, some Italian make nobody had ever heard of, more toy than car, and just as breakable.

From Jed's phonograph in the next room, she heard the happy lilt of Havanah G'ilah. Jed had played it a hundred times a day in the past two weeks, dancing to it with that funny, entranced grin on his pixie face. He was four years old and he believed in magic. Having discovered that the little black figures in books were there to speak to him, he had begun to teach himself to read. He already knew numbers because telephones enchanted him. When he learned that if you fed a particular sequence of numbers into one of them, it would evoke the actual voice of a real person, a grandparent, a cousin, he had memorized all their numbers and was as reliable as the telephone book. But the greatest magic, the most enthralling, was music. Before he could talk in sentences. he was picking out tunes on the piano. One day, he climbed onto the piano bench and, not banging with the flat of his hands, as babies do, he sounded first one note, then another, listening, exploring, while Ann held her breath in the doorway, watching him unravel the mystery of what the piano was about. It took him only a few minutes. Then, unerringly, he played *Twinkle, Twinkle Little Star.* When she came into the room to hug him, her prodigy, her Mozart, he looked up at her, his big, dark eyes excited and glowing with delight, then turned back to the piano, forgetting her at once. She thought she could see, then, the man he would become, and tried not to hate the woman he would marry.

She turned from the window and stretched, considering the day ahead. There was so much to do: the garden, closets, putting away winter clothing, going to the bank so that she could market for the weekend. Nick's summer camp had sent the clothing list and she had all that to shop for, and clothes for Jed's day camp, and the endless name tapes to sew. She was a slow, messy seamstress; maybe that was something Cory could do.

In the bathroom, Herbie had taped a note to the medicine chest mirror, the infallible bulletin board, reminding her to take the Dodge in to have the oil changed. After school, Nick would need to be driven to baseball practice. In spite of the promising scent of the new morning, it would be a day like all the others.

Jed came in while she was brushing her teeth and sat on the closed toilet seat.

"Wanna play haircut?" he asked.

"No."

"Yes you do. I'm the barber. You need a haircut." He waved his plastic clippers and said "Zzzzz." She had bought him the barber set because he was afraid of haircuts.

"Here's a toothpaste kiss," she said, leaning toward him.

He giggled. "No, you can't kiss the barber." She rinsed and hung away the toothbrush, then lifted him and kissed first one cheek, then the other. Though tall for his age, he weighed nothing. He was all bones, velvety skin, airy grace. She adored everything about him: the way he moved, the way he used his hands and held his head, the things he said, the voice he said them in, the ways his face changed to reflect every thought. She loved him so much that sometimes it felt like pain. So many kinds of love. The love for Nick, who had grown out of babyhood and into boyhood, so that you could see the qualities that had taken hold and would last his lifetime, his sweetness and gentle goodness. He was direct and honest and tolerant, bewildered by any other kind of behavior. He was handsome, like Herbie, and sometimes she had to keep from confusing him with Herbie, from the unfairness and inaccuracy of thinking of him as Herbie's and Jed as hers.

So many kinds of love. Last night she'd finished reading *Between the Acts* and begun *The Waves*, and realized that she was in love with Virginia Woolf. Later, she and Herbie had made love, trying to bury the unpleasantness earlier in the evening, when they'd had dinner in town with Arnold Werner, an account executive for a cigarette account Herbie was wooing.

"He said they'd never used such a small agency," Herbie told her at the bar, where they were waiting for the Werners to arrive. "When we get your account, I told him, we'll no longer be a small agency."

"I don't think you should do it," Ann said. "How can you seduce people into smoking now that we know how many of them it will kill?"

"Oh, please! They're going to smoke anyway, so why not Frontiers?"

The company was launching a new, longer, still deadlier cigarette. The thrust of Herbie's campaign was not to ignore the danger but, by implication, to court it. He had proposed the name, Frontiers, "the cigarette for the bold." The ads would depict adventurers at the moment of conquest, the hunter with a booted foot resting on the carcass of a dropped rhino, the climber planting a flag on the lonely summit of a frozen mountain, a soaked and bedraggled woman on a raft, the perilous rapids behind her, all of these daredevils exhausted, triumphant, and lighting up.

"You'll do anything for a buck," she said.

"You sit there smoking and tell me . . ."

"Yeah, I hate myself. But it's only me I'm killing."

"You're so unfair. This is the biggest thing I've ever
. . . oh, there they are."

She sat on, draining her drink, wishing there was time
for another, and watched him shoulder his way through the
standees at the bar. She dreaded the evening ahead. Through
the gloom, she watched Herbie at the checkroom helping
Cora Werner off with her coat, shaking Arnold Werner's
hand, all his movements fluid. Manhood had filled him out,
broadening him, without robbing him of the physical grace
that he'd passed on to his sons.

Those evenings! What torture they were for her, like
that first one back in the army days with the major, what was
his name, the one who'd wanted them to settle in Memphis.
When she tried to explain to Herbie why she hated these occasions, the pretense of interest, friendship, with people you
were with simply because of money, he told her that real life
was like that, you often had to do things you didn't particularly relish, he had to do them every day. But she knew he
really loved doing what he did. What's more, he said, you
never knew where new friends would come from; she might
even find that she could genuinely like some of these people.

She went down to breakfast. Jed zizzed his clippers
up and down her neck while she drank her coffee and read
The Times. She could hear Cory in the living room, fero-
ciously pummeling sofa cushions.

"Let's go to the zoo," Ann said, suddenly inspired.
"Would you like that, babe? How would you know, you've
never been."

"Yes I have."

"Central Park. That's just a little zoo. With cages.
We'll go to the real zoo."

"Don't they have cages in the real zoo?"

"No. Some."

"Why don't the animals run away?"

"They can't. They look free, maybe they even feel free, but they aren't." Like me, she thought. No cages, fences, ditches, moats. But ties. Emotional ties. The needs of others. Her own, too. Needs, boundaries. Yes, the zoo. Back in time for Nick, but the hell with all the rest.

They began with the seals, then proceeded to the children's zoo where Jed, grinning nervously, passed among the ducks and geese and rabbits, pausing to touch them tentatively, gently. She watched him, the sun warm on her back. The air here was different, heavier, weighted with feral redolence and with something more, something ineffable and disturbing, something she couldn't name.

Small children scampered everywhere, children with mothers, with nursemaids, in groups with teachers. It was a weekday and there were almost no men, so that when one appeared she noticed him, and then, with an overwhelming rush of emotion, recognized him. Jake. She turned away, hoping he hadn't seen her, and waited for her blood to subside. Jake.

She turned for another look, to make sure, and yes, it was Jake. He had twin girls in tow, pretty little urchins with long, streaky yellow hair, wearing blue jeans. Seeing in them the woman Jake had married, she felt a stab of jealousy. But how was it possible that Jake was just as she remembered him? The last time she'd seen him was, what, fifteen years ago, a few months before her marriage, the night before he shipped out, when they'd assured each other that the war would end soon (they didn't believe it; the war would never end), and, loving each other as they did, the waiting would be bearable. "My roots are in your pocket," he'd told her, and she cried and assured him that they were safe there, and precious. She had never loved anyone more, yet a few months later, weeping bitterly, she wrote to say that she was going to be married this coming Saturday. If she had broken any part of his heart, she had broken her own, too, not only for the loss of him, but for that incomprehensible failure in herself, for the glimpse of her crippler, that mute, willful creature locked within, the real boss, who moved her in ways that seemed to have nothing to do with her feelings or her intellect, whose logic she wouldn't begin to understand until so much later, on Kantfogel's couch.

"I missed him for years," she told Kantfogel.

"Mmm?"

"He scared me. Herbie was easy. Jake was, I don't know, too real."

"How, too real?"

"I felt more in control with Herbie." Control. She had grown up powerless in her father's house. But Jake hadn't been anything like her father. "There were so many reasons," she said. "Too many. Jake came from a poor family. Everything was a struggle for him. His education. Every other semester off, working to pay for the next semester. And the work he did . . . organizing sharecroppers in the south, getting beaten up, nearly starving. He'd buy a cup of tea in a cafeteria where you could help yourself to free packets of saltines. He'd load the tea with sugar and milk and pile catsup on the crackers. That was a meal. His future was so uncertain. He was going back to school after the war for his doctorate so he could teach. Literature, he was literary, he wrote poems."

"Like you."

"My parents didn't like him. He was so silent with them, though not because of shyness. He honestly couldn't find anything to say to them. But because of me, he was interested in them, in observing them, observing me with them, like an anthropologist in some unknown, primitive society. My parents didn't know what to make of him, so they made fun of him. My father never trusted intellectuals. If they're so smart, he always said, how come they're not rich? Jake, he said, was a loser. I half believed him. I'd never had experience trusting my feelings. And then, well, control."

Control.

"Colitis," Kantfogel said, dangling the word between them. Colitis. Yes, loss of control.

"When I'm trapped," she said. "In the middle of a long row at a concert. In tunnels. In traffic. In stalled elevators. In a classroom. Then I panic. Fear of being trapped. No, fear when I'm trapped that I'll lose control. And do what? I get terrible stomach cramps. Fear that I won't be able to hold it, that I'll shame myself in front of strangers. Do we have to go back to toilet training?"

Shame. My body, unlike yours and yours and yours, contains this *dreck*, and if it can't contain it I'll be exposed as the vile creature I am.

"It can't be the shit, though, can it? I have a recurrent toilet dream."

"Ah?"

"I wish you wouldn't say 'ah?' It's annoying."

"The dream."

There are variations, but essentially it's that I need a toilet and the only available one is public and filthy and stinking, the floor flooded with urine, often with turds floating in it. Sometimes I'm barefoot. Compulsion, revulsion.

Need, of course, wins. I'm on the toilet, trying to keep my feet out of the muck, the piss. There's no privacy. Strangers everywhere. Trapped and shamed by my need, I want out. And I can't do what I have to do."

She turned onto her side, fighting tears of self-loathing. Think!

"So many layers. The physical, that first lesson: re-press the need, contain it, direct it. Don't react instinctively, spontaneously. Control yourself. Suppress, repress, don't, for God's sake, express. That first lesson with the sphincter, and all the lessons then and later, all the orifices, those natu-ral openings through which we not only receive but spill. The waste products, the physical garbage. Later, the waste products of our feelings, the excesses. Don't cry, blow your nose, control your temper, don't vomit on your shoes. Shit goes out the cellar door, emotions rise like vomit and spill out of your face."

"Another fancy essay. I wouldn't describe you as over-controlled, Ann. On the contrary, glib."

"Shamed by my need, I can't do what I have to do," she said slowly, quoting herself. "I think in those toilet dreams, all the strangers are women. But why wouldn't it be all women? It's the Ladies Room."

"Why don't you talk about your mother?"

"There's nothing to say about her."

"Nothing? That's saying a lot."

"Nothing that I haven't already said, I mean."

"Here you're allowed to repeat yourself."

She was silent for a while, wondering what to begin with. The beginning. "In the beginning," she began, "like all mothers. . ."

"Never mind all mothers."

". . .she was at the heart of everything. Toweringly important. I can still remember how I felt, and I must have been an infant, how a room changed when she came into it, how much was missing when she was gone from it. She was the only one who could give me comfort or praise so that it counted. The source. The first love, certainly, and probably the one no other could match. I couldn't tell where she left off and I began. The womb and the cord. That's all very normal, right?"

"Normal, shnormal."

"But normal, shnormal is what we're talking about. Normal people don't shit in public."

"Do you?"

"So why is there always the fear that I might? What is this fear of being exposed, of being uncontained, of being out of control? Of being . . . different?"

Other women. Why should they fit so neatly and she not? Was she a lesbian? Kantfogel would groan if she brought it up again. He would say, "There's nothing in your Rorschach, nothing in your dreams, nothing in your history." He would say, "Why don't you go to bed with a woman, already, and get it out of your system?" He refused to take it seriously. It was an evasion, like everything else she brought to him. But what could she be evading more serious that that?

"I did once," she said.

"Go to bed with a woman?"

"Shit in my pants. Soil myself. I was about six. Playing outside. The doors were all locked. The front door, the back door. Bridget was in the basement doing laundry."

"Bridget?"

"The maid. Anyhow, I banged on the side door and screamed and wept and then I couldn't hold it anymore."

"What did you feel?"

"Shame. Disgust. Rage."

"Ah, rage."

"I was locked out. Of my own house."

"You didn't have the key?"

"No. The only key I ever had was my skate key. Not the key to the house."

Now I have the key, she thought. I'm a big girl now.

"Where was your mother?"

"Not home. She was never home."

"So who were you mad at?"

"Bridget. I wanted to kill her."

"Not your mother?"

"My mother wasn't home. I told you."

She was weeping. She couldn't imagine why.

"Growing up is like falling out of love," she said. "Beginning to see the faults, the flaws. Becoming critical so that you can become separate." She blew her nose. "Still, it's painful and confusing. My mother was beautiful and clever and intelligent. She had a million friends who were crazy about her. Still has. In school, she was popular, promising, the most likely to succeed. Sometimes when we were together, going somewhere, she'd run into one of her old schoolmates and I'd see the excitement in their eyes when they recognized her, with what awe they greeted her. I'd feel proud. But as I grew older, there was no way I could connect what she'd been with who she was."

"Who was she?"

"She played cards all the time. Even at parties, they played cards, the men in one room, the women in another.

They never just sat around and talked. What could they have to say to each other? She read books, nothing too demanding, and the newspaper, and The Ladies Home Journal, did crossword puzzles, went to theater, movies, out to dinner. But it was all the same. All entertainment. A way of getting through the days, time, life, painlessly. Killing time. My mother did what was necessary to keep the house running, but there were always cooks, cleaning women. The worst thing was that she let my father tyrannize her. She was completely subservient to him. She threw away her own life, but she was no different from her friends. They'd been raised to be like that, mothers, wives of successful husbands. Their own mothers were peasant women who'd emigrated from eastern Europe to work in sweatshops. What more could they want for their daughters than that they be rich and idle?"

Ann remembered how, almost daily, she'd vowed that she would never be like that. "When I swore that I'd never live an unexamined life, that I would at least try to do something meaningful, they made fun of me. Who did I think I was?

"Their notion of humor, especially my father's, was mockery, denigration. I'd better learn something useful because what man would ever want to support me. Support, he said, not live with, not marry, certainly not love. Support. I don't think he ever said a kind or approving word to me. Or to anyone else."

Yet her mother wasn't neurotic or unfulfilled. She was perfectly satisfied. As a woman, she'd passed with flying colors. Of course, she hated his bullying and yelling, his anger, and often it made her cry for a few minutes, but the least she could do was suffer that. "He's a difficult man," she would say. But he was more than difficult. He was selfish, megalomaniacal, full of hatred and rage, and he had all the power.

"Naturally, I couldn't be like my mother, but how did I know it? I did, though, very early, I think by the time I was three." Still, growing up, she'd often been tormented by doubt.

"God, the absolute hell of being thirteen, fourteen, fifteen. I was skinny, gangling, a tomboy. I never felt comfortable in my clothes. My posture, my walk, were disgraceful, too flamboyant in action, slothful in repose." Her mother: Stand up straight. I don't know what to do with your hair. Why can't you carry yourself like a lady instead of a giraffe. Stop sprawling. The minute you put on a new dress it looks like a rag. You're getting your father's nose.

Her father: Can't you do something about her? Does she have to look like that? She'll never get a husband, I'll have her on my hands the rest of my life. She'd better learn typing. She's getting my nose.

Though far from insensitive, she'd learned to discount much of their estimate of her, wounding though it was. She had only to survey her contemporaries in gym class, tumbling on mats, hanging from rope ladders, perspiring at volleyball, to be reassured. She was no freak. She wasn't fat or smelly or hairy, her complexion was clear, her coloring good, her eyes bright, large and uncrossed, her bones straight, her bite perfect. She hadn't required orthodontia, eyeglasses, or orthopedic shoes. She didn't need diet doctors, salves, ointments, Tasty Yeast, special tutors, or even psychological counseling.

"When I summed it all up, I felt my parents had gotten a bargain in me, but there was no way to convince them. For a daughter, they had some other picture in their head."

"Glib," Kantfogel said. "For a minute there, you were doing all right. Tell me, when did you stop feeling your feelings and get so glib?"

"If I stopped feeling my feelings, what am I doing here?" But it was an interesting question. She'd always thought of glibness as a sword: parry, thrust, touché, etc. Now she saw that it was, indeed, a shield.

"The minute you think about your feelings, they begin to change," she said.

"Exactly."

"What's the point of trying to translate feelings into words? All you're doing is changing them into ideas."

"That isn't all you're doing."

"Okay, so the point is to recognize and understand them in order to master them. But that's still thought and will, no longer feeling."

"No longer inappropriate feeling."

"Isn't that judging feelings? Arguing with them? Go away, anger, you're too excessive for the occasion. Love, you're not love, you're need. And you, fear, you're really anger. Or vice versa."

"It's listening to your feelings, and understanding where they're coming from."

"I wanted to talk about Jake. It's impossible to stick to the subject here!"

"You are the subject."

She had met him at Belle's wedding. Belle was her best friend and she and Walter were being married beneath a *chupah*, a portable canopy held above them by four poles, as if to protect them from the direct rays of the God they didn't believe in, but in whose eyes they were nonetheless being joined by a rabbi. The ceremony was for the old people, the family, for whom the marriage wouldn't be a marriage if it were performed in any other way.

Ann's attention was focussed totally on the ceremony. She was interested and moved by it. Still, some peripheral part of her was intensely aware of a young man at the other end of the crowded living room, a soldier in a neatly pressed private's uniform. Later, Ann would wonder what had made her so conscious of him, since there was nothing exceptional about him. He wasn't even the kind of man she thought of as her "type." It was as if he were sending messages to her, and later he told her he was doing just that. Even so, it had taken two weeks of persistent courtship on his part before, slumped one evening beside him on a sofa in the living room of friends of his, sleepy from too much wine and heavy talk, she had looked up at his profile, at the long curl of his eyelashes, at his sweet, serious mouth through which he spoke with such oddly precocious profundity. How fine he was, how sensitive and perceptive and wise. She felt an overpowering rush of warmth and tenderness and lust. She had just that moment fallen in love with him.

"Let's go," she had said, pressing his arm. She couldn't wait to get out of there, to be alone with him. To tell him. It was as if she had swallowed some powerful potion. "Now. I want to go." She was being rude. He looked at her, surprised. They had been talking about Jake's poems. He had just published six of them in a university quarterly. She thought they were wonderful. She had never told him that she wrote, too, but now she needed to tell him. She was a closet poet. She needed to tell him that, everything. She wanted him to tell her everything, too, the color of his mother's eyes, whether his father had been loving, if he had cried his first day at school, how many women he had loved, if he could name trees, birds, mushrooms. "Please, let's go," she said again, not caring that she was being rude. He looked at her and smiled. It was such a slow, thoughtful smile, how was it she hadn't seen it before? "I'm so tired," she lied. A few minutes earlier it would have been true. Now she felt as though she might never need to sleep again.

As soon as they were outside in the cold winter night, she said, "Jake, I love you. It's so strange. I'm frightened. I *really* love you."

He caught her arm and turned her to face him.

"Is that why . . .?"

"I couldn't wait another minute to be alone with you, to tell you."

"But . . ."

"I know. I don't know. I just suddenly knew it."

"Are you . . .?"

"Absolutely. I didn't know it in my head. I kept on not knowing it in my head. Then suddenly there it was, in my gut."

"Your gut?" He laughed.

"My heart. I mean it's visceral. I don't know what I mean. Let's take a taxi."

He held her close and kissed her with great tenderness, then drew back to look at her. He was so serious. He looked so happy, but in such a grave way. Then, releasing her, he turned three perfect cartwheels, coming to his feet with a flourish ten yards away, beneath a lamp post in whose light she saw that it had begun to snow.

"I didn't know you could do that," she called, catching a fat wet snowflake on her tongue."

"I can do anything."

A month later, he was gone. For three months they wrote every day. He wrote long, beautiful letters, letters she would never be able to throw away, even after he had told her that he had ceremoniously burned all of hers. His letters were in a box somewhere at the back of a closet shelf, more of her effects for someone else to dispose of.

"And yet," she told Kantfogel, "at that very same time I was half in love with this woman. Nell."

She waited for Kantfogel to groan, to snort with impatience. He was silent. Perhaps he was asleep.

"Well, I am two people," she argued, as though he had spoken. "I can lead a perfectly normal life, with all the normal feelings." Normal? Was that the right word? "But there's this other part of me that's just as real."

"Everyone is a little bisexual," he said, making it into the common cold, a mild allergy. "Androgynous." But she didn't believe it, or if she did, it was meaningless. She wanted to talk about it. She was afraid to talk about it.

"Nell," she said.

She had indeed learned to type. She dropped out of school and got a job in a luxurious Madison Avenue penthouse, home and office of Madame von Kirstenstiel. "Call me Madame," the woman said, and Ann laughed, and called her Madame. She was a baroness who had begun life as Sally Wiggins of Atlanta, Georgia. Although widowed, she remained wedded to the late baron's title. She published and did most of the writing for a highly profitable, syndicated newspaper column called The Global Gourmet. Ann's job as an apprentice writer was to plagiarize, as artfully as possible, recipes culled from the hundreds of cookbooks in Madame's singularly one-dimensional library, rewriting the text without altering ingredients or preparation, and including as often as possible the brand names of the subscribing advertisers' products. Madame had what she called a "personalized style." The recipes were required to speak in her distinctive voice, breezy and humorous, yet with the sophistication and dignity befitting her title. Imitating voices was no problem for Ann, who had written in so many of them during the years of her Endless Novel.

But now Ann was a professional writer, paid a not bad salary, although she was soon bored to death. Still, after two months her salary was raised even more. She was already earning as much money as most of the young 4F men she knew. Two other women lived in the penthouse with Madame, one of them her aged mother, a wraith in widow's weeds who lurked, like a stray from a Greek chorus, speaking always in stage whispers. The other woman was Nell Parsons, a mysterious woman who was in charge of production, a woman of indefinite age and pale, faded beauty, remarkable for her dramatically thrilling speaking voice, a voice controlled by a disciplined apparatus of such perfection that it hardly mattered to Ann what she said. On the rare occasions when she was moved to speak, each word was a jewel, perfectly formed and modulated, deeply vibrant. Ann was entranced. She soon found herself trying to imitate Nell's voice. If she could learn to speak that way, naturally, without having to think about it, her whole life, she was sure, would change.

Not that Nell Parson's life was enviable. In fact, she was desperately unhappy.

Late one afternoon, near quitting time, Ann was in the kitchen, learning from Nell how to make a perfect Scotch Old Fashioned, Madame's cocktail of choice, which they were more and more frequently invited to share with Madame at the working day's close. It was one of the job's increments. When properly trained, Ann was expected to assume the task of bartender.

"If you have to grind the sugar cube with that cunning little pestle," she asked, "why not use ground sugar in the first place?"

"Because," Nell said, "the sugar cube must absorb the bitters before being ground."

"That's ridiculous," Ann said, unconvinced.

"There's a right way and a wrong way. We have a reputation to uphold." There was a faint edge to Nell's voice, enough to hint that, at least in the matter of sugar cubes, she might be on Ann's side.

They drank at five. At five-thirty, after one drink, Ann departed.

"How lucky you are to be able to leave," Nell said, seeing Ann glance at the clock on the kitchen wall. It was the first time she had said anything personal to Ann.

"Why? Can't you leave?"

"She has things for me to do at all hours of the day and night. I'm at her beck and call."

"But why must you be?" Ann asked. She couldn't imagine anyone being so devoted to Madame.

"Some day I'll tell you about it," Nell said, sighing, and then went on to tell her. "I suppose I ought to be grateful, and in a way I am. This job has literally saved my life." She paused to stab out the remains of a cigarette she had abandoned in an ashtray next to the Scotch. "I'd spent two years in my apartment in total isolation until a mutual friend of mine and Madame's persuaded me to take this position. In those two years, I spoke to no one except on the telephone to Gristede's, to the delivery boy, and to this one friend, when she called. Otherwise, there was no one but Toulouse."

Toulouse was her mynah bird, a raucous creature who was often permitted to fly free. When he did, the bird screeched and swooped onto Ann's head, its powerful claws tangling in Ann's hair, while she froze with terror, and with anger at Nell, who found this amusing. Had Ann been less paralyzed with fear, she might have killed the bird.

She thought of Nell cloistered for two years with that dreary bird, who had been taught by an earlier owner to say only "impossible," and of what Nell's apartment must have been like. Once, sent to fetch some papers from Nell's bedroom, Ann was surprised by its disorder and chaos, which seemed so at odds with a woman whose diction was so precise. The bureau was littered with tobacco crumbs, spilled face powder, hairpins, unsheathed lipsticks, a soiled comb and brush tangled with hair. Clothing was strewn across the floor and the unmade bed, and on a chair there was a limp jumble of deflated stockings that, unwashed, retained the ghostly shape of Nell's legs.

"Why?" Ann asked. "Why did you live that way?" She saw that Nell's eyes had the ruined look of one who weeps too much. Despair. A despair so profound could exist only to fill some awful vacuum. "What had you lost?"

Nell, slicing an orange, stopped with the knife poised, and stared at Ann, startled, then slowly smiled. It was the first time Ann had seen her smile.

"My, you are intelligent," she said, "for one so young."

They became friends. During the lunches Ann persuaded Nell to take with her at neighborhood restaurants (she had rarely ventured out of the apartment in the years she had been there), she learned Nell's story. She had been married, at first blissfully happily, to a brilliant young man of enormous promise, gradually ruined by drink. He had been the great love of her life, but she came to hate and fear him, a bad drinker, violent and tireless. Toward the end, Nell took to locking herself in the bathroom, had spent many nights trying to sleep on the cramped bathroom floor, or in the tub, while he raged and tried to knock down the door, needing a target for his insane rage. Until that final night when, after weeping for hours, pleading for Nell to come out, he had gone into the bedroom and shot himself. When she came out, his blood and brains, his useless, brilliant, ruined brains, were all over the wall and ceiling.

"I could have saved him," she said, weeping into her chicken salad. "I should have saved him."

"You couldn't have saved him," Ann said, with that arrogant assuredness the young use for wisdom. The story thrilled her. She had never known anyone who had lived through anything as dramatic. She couldn't imagine anyone she knew killing himself. They were far too ordinary, commonplace, normal. Nell was straight from the pages of a novel and Ann was having lunch with her.

"Why do you say that?" Nell asked.

"How could you have saved him? You were his wife."

"What does that mean?"

"He was your husband and he nearly destroyed you."

"Are you saying that it was because I was his wife?"

"He was sick. A doctor might have cured him, but not you. He must have seen you as part of his problem. He chose you, married you, used you. For his own sick purposes. To feed his failure. To have you to blame, to stand in for whatever it really was. To help him destroy himself."

What did she know? She was making it up as she went along. She was a novelist, embroidering the plot.

"Then I shouldn't have allowed myself to be used," Nell said. "In that way, I failed him."

"How could you not have allowed it? You weren't even aware of it."

"Why wasn't I? How are you aware of it?"

"I wasn't in it."

How grown up, how sure, how strong she felt. In the weeks that followed, they lunched on this conversation and variations of it, many times, and Nell's guilt was gradually swept away by the force of Ann's relentless common sense and energy, such ordinary dross, annealed by Nell's need into gold. Ann felt herself grow taller, stronger, felt her own power and, with it, gratitude to Nell for giving her this new, additional Ann she could admire. It made her greedy. It only remained to rescue Nell from bondage to Madame, to help her regain some sense of herself so that she could begin to come alive again. A simple task. She set about it at once.

"Control," she told Kantfogel years later. "I was in control, the one with power."

She pored over the classified ads. Without telling Nell, she went to look at several available apartments before finding the perfect one, a furnished sublet under the Fifty-Ninth Street bridge with river views and old-world elegance.

"Call this number," she told Nell. "And arrange to see it."

"What do you mean?" Nell said, when she understood what Ann had done. "I could never leave here. She'd be furious."

"Nonsense. You can handle it. You'll remind her of your gratitude, and tell her how important the work is to you, but that now, thanks to her, you feel healed enough to live in your own place. She'll be relieved."

Nell fell in love with the apartment, as Ann knew she would. "It's beautiful," she said. It was Scotch Old Fashioned time again, and Ann was mixing the drinks. The winter sun, low in the west, streamed into the room, burning Nell's hair copper. Her small, delicate hands, the knuckles white, gripped the back of a kitchen chair. "I'm not sure I can manage the rent." She could easily afford it. "The thought of packing."

A few days later, Ann was helping Nell gather up the few things she had brought from her past life: books, the bird, a tennis racket, an ancient portable typewriter, her few clothes. There were other things in storage. But why the tennis racket, Ann wondered. Given the circumstances, it was incongruous until Ann saw it as a kind of talisman; Nell had intended all along to survive.

At the end of the week, they moved into the apartment under the bridge. Ann had offered to pay a small part of the rent in exchange for being allowed to stay there occasionally. She was living with her parents and there was no reason in the world why she should share Nell's apartment, except that it gave Nell the final needed push. Ann thought of it as a ploy, but she also hoped it would be a way for her to begin to leave home.

Home was the ten room apartment on Central Park West. Girls of her age and class weren't expected to leave home unless they were away at school (she had gone to school on the subway), or married. What was the point? Where would she be as comfortable? She had her own bedroom and bath, and a little study with a working fireplace. All the privacy a girl could want unless, as her father said, she was up to no good. There were a cook and a chambermaid at home, and Ann's only responsibility was to throw her worn clothes into the bathroom hamper, and put them back in the bureau drawers when they returned, laundered and pressed.

She told her mother about Nell and what a triumph it would be to get her out of Madame's clutches. Nell was like an invalid, however, and would need help for a while. Her mother was sympathetic, and they joked about Ann having a *pied a terre* she could get to on the crosstown bus.

"This is your place," she told Nell. "We're not sharing it. Of course I don't want the bedroom, it's your bedroom. That is your bed." Nell laughed with pleasure while Ann watched to see what laughter did to her face. The grief lines were permanent scars.

There was no doorman, so they carried everything up in several trips. When they had it all inside and the door closed and locked, they stood in the foyer in their coats, grinning at each other. Nell breathed a long sigh, then put her arms around Ann and gently rested her cheek against Ann's.

"I'm so happy," she said. "Did God send you to me?"

"God, no!"

They had brought along a bottle of Scotch and they made drinks and toasted their absent host, a wealthy Italian bachelor who had been parachuted somewhere behind the lines to fight in the underground. They drank to his bravery and to his excellent taste, going though the apartment, examining everything in detail. The living room was monastic, medieval, with hand carved tables and chairs of oak, blackened by time, with frayed purple velvet chair covers. There were tapestries, rugs, a fireplace, no lamps. Instead, there were heavy iron *torchères* holding fat white candles. Nell lit the candles and turned off the electric lights on the ceiling and walls, throwing the room back a few centuries, turning it even more mysterious and awesome. They sipped their drinks in silence, feeling that they were in their host's ancestral palazzo, seated among his ghosts. A radiator began to knock, breaking the spell.

"I'm famished," Ann said.

They had a picnic supper: bread, cheese, a roast chicken, wine. Nell unpacked the food and set the table with the delicate Venetian wine glasses and festive Tuscan pottery dishes from the kitchen cabinets, while Ann fiddled with a radio that she'd discovered lurking in the shadows. The room filled with music.

"Mozart, too," Nell said, happily.

The candles flickered. The room was warm, alive, yet Ann had a sense of unreality, as if they were children playing, or actors on a stage. Nell poured the wine and held her glass up to the light, turning it into a jewel.

"To the first supper," she said.

"To your new life."

"To our new life," Nell said, looking at Ann with love. Ann felt a tremor of fear, and, with it, an impulse to smash the moment, to say something vulgar, something cruel. She tore off a chicken leg and bit into it.

That night, lying on the narrow sofabed she'd made up in the living room, she watched the shifting geometry cast on the ceiling by the lights from the cars crossing the bridge, waiting for sleep to overtake her. She heard Nell stirring in the bedroom. After a while, the bedroom light went on and Nell, in a long nightgown, was silhouetted in the doorway.

"Are you asleep, Ann?" she asked softly.

Ann held her breath, then said, "No."

"I can't sleep," Nell said. "I'm too happy to be alone. Come sleep with me."

"You'd never fall asleep with me in there," Ann dithered. "I'm a tosser and turner."

"Just for a minute. Just be with me."

Ann got up and followed Nell back to her bed and slid in beside her. Nell put out the light and took Ann's hand, lacing their fingers together. They lay quietly, not speaking, watching the lights on the ceiling. Nell turned, and Ann felt her breath on her cheek.

"In the East," Nell said, "when you save someone's life, they don't say, 'I owe my life to you.' They give it to you." Her mouth was so close to Ann's ear that her words fluttered like the wings of butterflies. "You've saved my life, Ann. What will you do with it?"

The idea alarmed Ann. She lay paralyzed, riven by opposing instincts. Was that what she wanted? That power? Or had she merely been tidying up? She loathed what she was feeling, but she loved it, too. She was excited and repelled. She was scared to death.

"I haven't saved your life," she said, stiffening. "Time did it. I just gave you the necessary shove. Such a small shove."

"No, Annie, it was more than that." She pulled Ann around to face her. "Hold me. I never thought I'd feel anything again, but I do. I can feel my blood, my skin, my nerve endings. For God's sake, Ann, hold me."

Ann put her arms around Nell, feeling the length of her against her own body, the softness of her breasts, her stomach. She closed her eyes, waiting for words to come. "It isn't me, Nell," she said, after a while. "What you're feeling has nothing to do with me." She forced herself to be a hundred years old, a wise old witch sitting in a tree. "What you feel is for yourself, for this place, for your new freedom, for the end of the bad time, for the sweetness of life."

"Yes, all that, but you, too. I love you, Ann."

"No, you've come back to loving yourself,   don't you see? And I happen to be here." Though she had already begun to suspect that love might always be that, chancy, the intersection of time, place, person, and readiness. "I'm just what happens to be in your line of vision." She laughed, trying not to feel the rising flood of physical desire. "And in your bed."

"Oh, Annie, it's you, it's you. It's your youth and your energy and your sweet funnyness. It's your eyes and the laugh lines that are already there, and your smile, and your toughness, and your vulnerability. And what I love most is that I can see how you're going to be when you really grow up."

"How am I going to be?" Ann asked, interested.

"Ah, now I've got your attention." Nell's laugh rippled down the length of Ann's body. Lightly, her lips brushed across Ann's. No, she mustn't, she wouldn't. "If they don't wreck you," Nell said, "you're going to be an absolute marvel."

They. The thought of her future released her from the present. She thought of Jake. Whatever this was, with Nell, it was too threatening, much too frightening. In any case, she would have had no idea how to go on with it.

"In a little while," she told Nell, "when you're more sure of yourself, you'll remember that not all men are violent. You'll stop being afraid of them and of your feelings." Chastely, she kissed Nell, then slipped out of bed. "You'll remember this as a momentary aberration, and what relief you'll feel!"

"I didn't know if I was acting out of wisdom or cowardice," she told Kantfogel. "Now I know it was both. It was wise of me to be frightened."

"Too bad you couldn't have gone ahead and gotten it out of your system," Kantfogel said.

"Oh, God, you're so predictable." Maybe she was coming to the end of her analysis. "If I could have handled my feelings then, I wouldn't be here now."

"I couldn't agree more."

It had all been there in that crucial year, all the choices, her confusion, her limitations, the sowing of the seeds of her breakdown.

And here she was, standing in the sun of a spring fifteen years into that time's future. The Bronx Zoo. With Jed, Herbie's child and hers, hoping that a man with twin girls, a dozen feet away, wouldn't see her.

But he did see her.

"Ann?" he asked, walking toward her, his face open with surprise and pleasure. "Is it really you?"

She smiled, feeling her color rise. "How are you, Jake? You look wonderful."

"My God."

"You look exactly the same, except for the clothes. I never saw you out of uniform." He wore a rumpled tweed jacket and baggy gabardine slacks, shirt open at the neck, no tie. "Your little girls are beautiful."

He smiled with pride. "Which one is yours?" he asked. She pointed to Jed, busy for some minutes past bolting and unbolting the door of a doll-sized Swiss chalet, empty of the guinea pigs it was supposed to house. As children filed past for a look, Jed swung the door open and said, "Nobody home," then shut it again and slid the bolt. He was having a very good time. "He's practicing to be a doorman when he grows up," she said.

Jake touched her sleeve. "How have you been, Ann?" he asked. She knew that what he meant was her life. He looked at her steadily, honestly wanting to know.

"Good," she said, too quickly. "Oh, Jake, not bad. A very average life." She gestured toward Jed. "Another of those at home, in school. Home is a split-level house on Red Maple Lane in Scarsdale." She laughed self-consciously, thinking of a man she knew who called all streets in suburbia Sparrow Fart Lane. "It isn't a lane at all, just an ordinary curving street, and I doubt if there's more than one red maple on it. Herbie has an advertising agency. I've stopped thinking of myself as a poet, even in secret. Instead, I'm in analysis, learning how to be a housewife and mother. Now you."

He had listened closely, not smiling. "I'm very happy," he said, and she knew it was true. Lucky Jake. "These are my youngest. There are three others. I'm on sabbatical, here for a few days visiting my mother."

"Where's home?"

"Cambridge. Harvard. Seventeenth century English literature."

"Just as you planned it. Good for you, Jake."

How unreal to be standing here, strangers, really, in that future they had once meant so desperately to share, exchanging their lives in this shorthand. The thousands of words that he had poured out from his deepest self were tucked away on a shelf in her bedroom, there on Red Maple Lane, and she had carried the memory of him around as part of her life. She probably always would.

Jed tugged at her sleeve. He wanted to move on, to see the "real" animals. So did she.

"Jake," she said, quickly, feeling she owed him something, "what I wrote you then was as honest, as true as I could make it at the time. It was incredibly painful for me. I want you to know that, even though I know that it's a long time since it mattered to you. I think one of the reasons I married Herbie was because I missed you so much. I was young and stupid and confused and it's taken me years and a fortune to begin to sort it all out."

She looked nervously past him at the blur of children, listening through their screams and laughter to the long silence that reverberated between her and Jake. Then he took her hand and held it.

"Thank you, Ann," he said.

"Goodbye, Jake."

"If you're ever in Cambridge. No, I mean that."

Jed tugged at her. She turned and they walked away, toward the lions, the tigers, the "real" animals, while she realized that what the air held that was heavier than air, was the screaming and preening and pacing, the turgid, swollen restlessness of this animal world in season, seeking and mating.

"Who was that?" Jed asked.

"Someone I once knew. A nice man."

"Don't you still know him?" Jed asked.

"No."

FIFTEEN (Now)

Minutes after being introduced to Arty Tannenbaum, I catch myself humming *Tannenbaum, My Tannenbaum*. It probably happens to him all the time. Embarrassed, I glance his way, hoping his reaction will reveal something, the kind of people he knows, his frame of reference, whether he has a sense of humor. But nothing. Maybe he hasn't heard.

He is fairly tall, and as spare and dry and brown as last year's oak leaf still clinging stubbornly to its branch. His teeth may well be his own; there are flashes of gold among them when he smiles his small smile. Considering his age, he's not bad looking. Then I remember, with what is becoming a familiar jolt, that I am fifty and menopausal, probably what he would consider too old for him. At 65, or whatever he is, in good health and wealth, he can have women half his age and probably does. He has more than kept his figure. I can tell that he's indifferent to food and probably a golfer. The lines at the corners of his eyes, I'm pretty sure, haven't been etched there by laughter or good humor, but by squinting into the sun after the long ball.

While I am surveying him so uncharitably, he is showering me with indifference. After the dry handshake, he turned to my father to ask about his pacemaker. My father undid his shirt and bared his chest to reveal the rectangular lump protruding under the skin near his breastbone. That done, and my father rebuttoned, the two men are discussing the market. The Steiners and the Sperbers, invited by my mother in the belief that the muddle of numbers would make her machinations less obvious to Tannenbaum, who could hardly care less, are talking about the lottery. A woman who lives in the same building as Flora Sperber's sister-in-law, has recently won the state's largest jackpot to date, twelve million dollars.

"So what would you do with it if it had been you?" my mother asks Flora.

"If I won twelve million dollars? At my age?" Flora says. "I'd kill myself."

They are all dressed informally, yet they've obviously taken pains, as always. The women wear slacks with coordinated print shirt jackets, chiffon kerchiefs knotted at their throats, and shoes that match some part of their outfit. Equally colorful and coordinated in slacks and blazers, the men's throats are bound by paisley ascots. Their slacks are rust, canary, kelly; Arty Tannenbaum's are marine, his blazer navy, his ascot several blues flecked with red. I unfocus my eyes and the room fills with a blur of gay tropical birds.

Florida. I wish I were home in the snow with my cat, missing Angie, wondering where she is, wondering if she's loving someone else, knowing that she's loving someone else, wishing I hadn't quit smoking, wishing that at any moment I'll be overwhelmed by a poem. I force myself to listen.

"If I didn't lay his clothes out for him every morning," Tina Sperber is saying of Fred, as though he were elsewhere, "he'd go naked." Fred looks at her lovingly through thick eyeglasses, and through his round, open mouth. "He's never admitted it, but I'm positive he's color blind." Tina is the strong one in that marriage. Fred makes jokes deadpan, moves slowly, has never made much money. Perhaps because of this, Tina's pose with him is one of perpetual, barely restrained exasperation. They've both been in and out of hospitals recently, she with heart and blood pressure, he with lungs and stomach, and they guard each other fiercely.

"I'll let you in on a little secret," Fred says to Tina. "I let you lay out my clothes on purpose. So you shouldn't feel completely useless."

"Ha, ha. I can live without such favors."

"Not the novie," he says, slapping her hand away from the smoked salmon. "You know it's too salty."

"I wouldn't even know what Irving has in his closet," Flora says. Irving has been her third husband for only two years. Everyone was surprised when she remarried so soon after Charlie's death. She idolized Charlie, who was handsome and adoring. "I never had to think about my Charlie's clothes. He had wonderful taste. I couldn't buy a dress without first modeling it for his stamp of approval." She sighs. "My Charlie. How I miss him. He never gave me a minute's trouble."

Irving, who is small and pudgy, nods amiably, his pudding face serene. He knew he was getting the leavings, a bargain he willingly made. He, too, adores Flora, who, at 76, is still slender, girlish, bubbly, sexy.

"Tell the truth," Fred says to Tina. "The first time I took you out, what was the main thing that impressed you? What a good dresser I was, right?"

Tina laughs, a big hearty laugh that grows and grows, her large body shaking.

"Oh, no," she gasps, barely able to speak. "The chry . . . the chry . . . the chrysanthemum." Her eyes fill with tears. She slaps her thigh. "In his lapel. He wore. Oh God. A big brown chrysanthemum."

"It was formal," Fred explains.

"A formal dance," Tina says. "His uncle was a cantor, so Fred knew about all the weddings. He'd ask his date if she wanted to go dancing, then get dressed up and crash the wedding. Complete strangers."

"I love to dance," Fred says, reasonably. "I could have been named for Fred Astaire, but he was too young. Anyhow, who knew? Everyone thought we were from the other side. Who could afford nightclubs?"

"That's how he courted me. A hundred weddings, at least, where we didn't know a soul."

"And then we decided to go to one where we knew everybody. That one we paid for."

"We're still paying."

"You know how Irving courted me?" Flora asks. "With poems."

"You're not the only poet around here," Irving tells me.

"Some day I'll show them to you," Flora says. "Henry Wordsworth Longfellow he's not, but they're really cute. I've got them all pasted up in a special album."

"I was too shy to talk to her in the beginning," Irving says. "My wife had been gone two years and Flora had just become a widow. I never thought I'd marry again, but I used to see her in the lobby and in the elevator and what could I do, I fell in love with her. So I began writing these poems and slipping them under her door. Only I didn't sign them."

"A complete mystery. I couldn't imagine who."

"Finally, after a month with a poem every day ,"

"Every single day without fail."

". . . the time was ripe. I wrote a poem to the effect if curiosity was killing the cat, tomorrow at 5:30 P.M. in the lobby by the mailboxes, the cat could gaze upon the gentleman so smitten, etcetera."

"You said I'd know you by your loving eyes and I did. But, no offense, what a disappointment. To look at you at first sight, Irving, even though I'd seen you around for years, wasn't to fall in love."

"I used to write poems, too," my father says. "When I was eleven, twelve, I delivered for my Uncle Julius's delicatessen. In those days, you sent the orders up in dumbwaiters, so it wasn't easy to get tips. I used to pin notes on the bags, poems like, 'I hope the pastrami brings you joy, but don't forget to tip the boy."

"Even his poems were about money," my mother says.

"You can see how useful poetry is," I say, feeling it's time I opened my mouth.

"You write poetry?" Arty Tannenbaum asks with a glimmer of interest.

"Sure," my father answers for me, suddenly proud. "She publishes them. Not that I understand them."

"They're not usually about money," I say. "Or pastrami."

"What are they about?"

"Everything else."

Tannenbaum reaches for a cracker, spreads chopped liver on it, tastes it gingerly. "Good chopped liver," he pronounces, then switches seats, sitting next to me.

"She made it," my mother says. "Ann makes the world's best chopped liver." Suddenly both my parents love everything about me.

"She's a very good cook," my father adds. This is true, but irrelevant. The way to Tannenbaum's heart is obviously not through his stomach. I'm beginning to feel like a hockey puck, with Tannenbaum the goal and my parents taking great, clumsy whacks at me, hoping to score.

"You really write poems?" Tannenbaum asks again, oddly interested. I nod.

"Why?" he asks.

Someone's cigarette is in an ashtray beside me. The smoke curls up directly into my nostrils. My hands flutter in my lap, little creatures, bird dogs trained to fetch cigarettes to my mouth. I fight to restrain them. Down, hands, down! I take a long swallow of Scotch.

"Why do you write poems?" Tannenbaum again asks.

"I'm not sure I understand the question," I say, sighing. Which particular why does he mean?

"I mean, what do you do? You go into a room and sit down at a desk?"

"Usually."

"Every day? And sit there how long?"

I can't imagine why I am having this conversation, but it's too late to cancel it. "A couple of hours in the morning," I say. "If it's going well, I go back to it after lunch. Or sometimes I wake in the night with something in my head, and I'll work until dawn, then sleep all morning. You never know when a poem may strike."

He listens with interest, watching my lips like a deaf man.

"Why does this interest you?" I ask. He brushes the question aside with an impatient gesture.

"Why do you do it? What makes you do it?"

"What makes anyone do anything?"

"You publish your poems in magazines?"

"Sometimes. Don't ask me which. You won't have heard of them."

"How much do they pay you?"

"I thought you'd never ask," I mumble. "Not much. Sometimes nothing."

"You mean: you'll work for a day, days, maybe more, on a poem, am I correct, and then let someone have it for nothing?"

Why is it that what seems so natural in my own world, not that I approve, always seems, even to me, freakish in this one? "And be happy they want it," I say.

His eyes narrow. "Don't you have any self-respect?" he asks.

What a rude question! "Money really doesn't have much to do with it," I say, feeling hopeless.

"I'm trying to understand," Tannenbaum persists, shaking his head, frustrated. "I want you to make me understand."

I can't help smiling. I like it that he wants to understand, no matter what's implied, and I know what's implied and it's simple. I am one of that species who doesn't behave according to the rules. He can understand thieves, he can understand murderers, but he can't understand poets. How can I even begin to explain it to him, that passion that's sometimes ecstasy, sometimes almost erotic, of struggling to shape this thing and of having it come out right? On what level, in what language, would it be possible to make Arty

Tannenbaum see it and know that it's important? "Well, why do people paint pictures?" I ask, still evading. "Or make sculpture? I do the same thing, but with words."

"You can hang a picture on a wall," my father says. "A statue can stand in a lobby, on a square, in a park. Decoration. But a poem? It sits on a piece of paper."

"So does music," I say, "until it's played. That doesn't mean it doesn't exist." I'm not even sure I believe it, but I persevere. "Once it's created it has its own life, even though it's meant to be read or heard or seen." Do the poems in my desk drawers have life? Does the mechanical act of printing a poem and then having it read by, at best, a few thousand people make it more real, more valid? I think of all the instantly forgettable, instantly forgotten, poems being written and published every year. I think about when I've died and poor Jed has to go through all the clutter in my drawers. I think about how, in the end, he'll scoop it all up and dump it into big, black plastic bags.

"You're talking about *what*," Tannenbaum says, "not *why*. Why do you do it? Why do *you* do it? What's in it for you?"

He isn't going to be put off. He really wants it, the answer. "It would take a long time," I mumble.

"I've got plenty of time. I'm retired."

From across the room where she's passing canapés, my mother darts a meaningful glance my way, smugly pleased that Tannenbaum and I seem to be hitting it off. See? she says with the merest quiver of an eyebrow, was I right or was I right? Next the ring, then no more worries about Ann, she'll be where every woman belongs: married. The years of my marriage don't count. I am not married now. I am unresolved, in limbo.

"How about dinner tomorrow night?" Tannenbaum asks. "So we can get to the bottom of this."

The room is suddenly silent. Everyone is waiting for my answer.

"All right, fine."

"There's a gala, an extravaganza, I think Tony Bennett, at the Diplomat. I'll reserve a table."

"Oh, no," I almost scream. "I couldn't." I cast about wildly for reasons. "I didn't bring clothes for anything like that."

My mother's laugh ripples across the room. "Don't be silly, Annie, you know perfectly well."

Accompanied by my mother the next morning through one mall after another, feeling malled to death, I am at last satisfactorily outfitted for my evening with Tannenbaum, a three piece silk pajama-like thing that I can't imagine wearing anywhere else in the world. My mother drapes jewelry wherever it will cling to me, and I'm all set.

At our commodious table for two, above the blare of the orchestra, we talk poetry.

"For starters," I say, tucking into the first course, gefilte fish *en aspic*, "let's talk about values, what we think is important. What do you do?"

He is poised over a shrimp cocktail, the largest shrimp I've ever seen, but his eyes are on me, glinting, almost hostile, as though he's waiting for some kind of attack.

"Me? I'm retired. I play golf. I have a boat. I fish. My wife died not long ago."

"What did you do before you retired?" I ask, though I know.

He picks up a knife and fork and slices one of the shrimp into manageable segments, dips one into a vat of cocktail sauce, and brings it daintily to his mouth. A revolving light-beam catches in his sharp brown eyes, on the inlay of a tooth, giving off sparks. He looks dangerous.

"A lot of things," he says, chewing slowly. "You could write a book. Most of my life I was in paper products, my father-in-law's business till he died, then mine. But you want to know the first real money I made? I made it transporting illegal booze for the Hassidim."

"The Hassidic Jews? They were bootleggers?"

"No, they made their own. It wasn't against their laws. They have their own laws."

"The Hassidic Jews with the big hats and the soft white hands? They had a still?"

"In the Catskills. They needed someone to drive the stuff back to Williamsburg, in Brooklyn. I was sixteen but tall and strong for my age. I've always been stronger than I look. Feel my arm." He waits for me to feel it. I feel it.

"Pure steel," he says, modestly. "They gave me a big Buick, it had a huge trunk, and I'd go up and help out for a day or two, then load up the trunk of the Buick with these big cans, they had turpentine labels, and drive it back. I could average a hundred bucks a week, big money in those days, especially for a kid."

"How long did that last?"

"Till they got caught. I'd been doing it for about a year, studying accounting a couple of nights a week." He takes another shrimp and chews, thoughtfully. "You know how they got caught?"

His look is sly, defying me to guess. I shake my head and smile, waiting.

"The still was in a *mikvah*. You know what a *mikvah* is?" I do, but he doesn't wait for me to say so. "A bath for

- 173 -

orthodox women. Where they go before they're married. It's a ritual."

"So they're clean for the bridegrooms," I say, to prove that poets aren't all dummies. "After their periods, too, so their husbands can have sex again without being *tref*, those pure, holy men."

"What are you, some kind of feminist? At your age? Listen, every religion has its . . . what's the word I want? Otherwise, how would you know it was a religion?"

"A *mikvah*," I say, loving the idea. "A still in a *mikvah*."

"Anyhow, to continue. Have you ever seen a still?"

"I'm afraid not."

"Well, when it's cooking, it generates a lot of heat. So. You know how, when you come into a little village in the winter and all the roofs are covered with snow? Well, what would you think if you happened to notice that one roof didn't have snow on it? Because, see, the heat of the still melted the snow on the roof of the *mikvah*."

"And that's how they got caught?"

"No, that's not how. Because they were smart, they thought of that. Just before dawn, when the roof had cooled down, the men would climb up ladders carrying pails of snow and they'd pack the snow onto the roof. Up and down, up and down, until the roof was covered."

I laugh and laugh. Those men in their beards and hats and long black coats scurrying up and down ladders by the dawn's early light with their pails of snow.

"Oh, wonderful," I gasp. "It's a musical comedy. 'Distillers on the Roof.'"

He grins, pleased at his success. "But how they got caught," he says, "was they got lazy. See, after you cook up

- 174 -

a batch, there's a residue, a mash. They were supposed to take it out and bury it, but in the winter it was hard work digging the frozen ground, so they began dumping it in a stream that ran behind the property. After a while, a lot of fish in a lake downstream began to die, and that's how they got caught. In the spring." He stabs another piece of shrimp and puts it in his mouth. "Listen," he says, "we came here to talk about why you write poetry."

"Right," I say, though I'd much rather keep him talking. "Did you have any heroes when you were growing up?" I ask, groping for a way to begin.

"Heroes?"

"Your father?"

"No, not my father, he was nothing. I guess any poor slob who made good."

"You mean, who got rich?"

"Yeah, who was successful. What about you?""

"Writers. I was a reader, and writers gave me the world."

He thinks for a moment, then nods. "Yeah, I can see that. If you weren't out in it, like I was, you had to get it from somewhere. Books."

"Even more important is the way I feel about language. In a more general sense, I mean. Do you really want to hear about this?"

"Yes I really do."

"Yes? Well," I swallow a mouthful of gefilte fish, giving myself time. "This is almost as good as my grandma's. So, let's begin at the beginning with man dragging himself up out of the slime . . ."

"What slime?"

"The primordial ooze. Whatever. First man. Way back." I push a sliver of fish around in its jelled broth, its slime. "In the beginning."

"Maybe it wasn't slime," he says, making a face. "Maybe it was the Garden of Eden."

"Try to imagine how it must have been, the terrific struggle to figure out how to survive. It's likely that man began with some primitive ape instincts and noises and a brain that grew more convoluted and complex the more he called upon it for help, and a body that grew less powerful and agile and hairy the more his brain gave him substitutes for muscle and hair and fangs."

Having nibbled his way through two of the shrimp, Tannenbaum pushes the plate away, finished. I look at the four remaining fat, pearly, prehistoric, foetal bodies, thinking what waste, what a long way we've come, indeed. I swallow the last of the gefilte fish.

""You're talking about evolution, right?" he asks, and I nod.

"In the beginning, just surviving took all man's energy. To keep from starving, freezing, being attacked by wild beasts, enemies. Why don't you finish your shrimp?"

"I wouldn't be able to eat anything else. You want them?" He pushes them toward me.

No thanks, " I lie. My cursed appetite. "Maybe one." I spear one with my gefilte fish fork. This seems to please him.

"Are you saying that because I was born poor, what was most important to me was to survive?"

"Yes. And it was." I know it from my father, that whole generation of immigrants and their children. "But I'm also talking about something else. As primitive man

- 176 -

evolved, he learned that there was strength in numbers. If he belonged to a group, a clan, he didn't have to do everything. Some hunted, some planted, some fought, some built, some made tools and weapons. What they invented, you see, was the community."

"I grew up in a community," he says, defensively. "I lived on Essex Street."

The waiter brings the soup as the orchestra breaks into a loud and lively medley of old tunes. Almost everyone gets up to dance.

"Why are you taking this personally? Of course you grew up in a community. And a family." I dip into my mushroom barley soup and see that he is watching the couples on the dance floor. Beneath the table, one of his tasseled black patent leather shoes taps to the rhythm of the music. He's bored.

"I'm boring you," I say.

"Come on! You were talking about the community."

"Okay. Now, think about those men, so close to animals, so newly evolved, poking and grunting and snarling and pointing and making sounds for whatever they wanted to say. The more they discovered the advantages of sharing, of cooperation, the more they must have felt their separateness, and their need to surmount it. They needed more and more sounds and facial expressions and gestures and inflections and tones of voice. They needed language."

A singer is blaring into the microphone. "Fooredeackasacky," he sings, "want some sea foooood, Mama." I laugh.

"Yeah, that's what they needed it for," he says, smiling. For the first time, I feel a barrier falling between us. We're almost companionable.

"Language, the greatest tool of all," I say. "Think what a miracle it was the first time someone pointed to the sky and said 'Rain,' in whatever language, and the people who were with him knew exactly what he meant and nodded their heads, and said, 'rain, rain.' And thereafter that was the word for it and when you heard the word you saw the rain in your mind, knew the wet of it, the smell of it."

He nods. "Okay, so people learned to talk," he says, finished after two spoonfuls with his *consomme printemps*. "So?"

"I'm trying to describe the magic of it, the sacredness, the wonder. For me, the most romantic thing about man is his development of this means of reaching out and conveying his own particular experience of life, his thoughts, his feelings, his wants, needs, observations. Wanting to speak of it. To share it. Wanting to hear it from others. And inventing the way." My soupspoon waves between us, emphasizing my passion.. Why am I doing this? Suddenly, I feel self-conscious, ridiculous. "This is embarrassing," I say.

"Why should you be embarrassed?" he asks, surprised. "When I was in paper products, I was never embarrassed to talk about it."

Paper, clean, necessary paper waiting to be written on, printed on, waiting for words. "What kind of paper products did you make?" I ask.

He grins. "Anything there is to wipe, we made a product for it. Mouth, nose, hands, asses. 'We wipe you clean.'"

"That wasn't your slogan? We wipe you clean?"

"In the beginning. Our first agency."

"That's the worst slogan I ever heard."

"That was my father-in-law. What did he know? Later, we got more dignified. We dropped it. We concentrated on softness and whiteness. We got a logo, an ivory castle up in the clouds. You've seen it. So go on. You were saying people talking to each other is romantic. I mean, I know I'm oversimplifying."

"What I'm speaking of is language that goes beyond, 'Danger!' 'Go away!' 'I need to mate,' 'It hurts,' 'Pass the salt.' I'm talking about a little girl, say, sitting in a cave watching her mother cry. Maybe her mother's in pain, maybe she's peeling wild onions. The little girl points to her mother's tears and says, 'Rain. Rain of the sad face.' Do you know what that little girl's done?"

"Forgotten the word for crying?"

"She's made a poem."

"That's a poem? Rain of the sad face? What is this with you and rain? Let's dance."

"There, you are bored."

"Not for a minute. I'm glued to your every word. But you still haven't told me why you write poetry."

The waiter hovers, filling the wineglasses, removing the soup, delivering the dinner plates which, unhelmeted, reveal Tannenbaum's steak, well done, no potatoes, a small green salad on the side; my pot roast, potato pancakes, stuffed derma, red cabbage, apple sauce.

"You like Jew food," he observes. I admit that unfortunately I like most kinds of food.

"I have explained why I write," I say, knowing that I've barely scratched the surface, and wondering again why I'm doing this, whether it's because I've once again mislaid my evanescent center here in this valley of the shadow of death.

"When people are starving," I say, taking a new tack, "there's only one thing they want: enough to eat. Once their basic needs are taken care of, they're able to want other things, to think of themselves in ways that are less basic. There's that other, almost bottomless self locked inside that can come out now. People want to make some sense of life, to pierce the darkness, to leave some record of their lives, their time. They think. They play. They invent music. They develop standards of beauty, of behavior, of morality. They become more and more concerned with the quality of life. All that, the learning to live together, the sharing, the telling and listening, the refining, is what we mean by civilization."

He looks at me shrewdly, chewing slowly. "Are you saying that poets are more civilized . . . are you telling me that you are more evolved than I am?"

"Oh, God, is that what I've said?" Yes, it is.

". . . because all you are, if you ask me, is more educated." Furious, he stabs his steak. "I may not be educated from books, but I've got plenty of street savvy. I got my education out there in the real world, where it counts. Put someone like you out there, you wouldn't survive for a week, you know that?" He's calm again; he's reassured himself.

"I'm sorry. I didn't mean any of this personally."

"Well that's the way it sounded. How come you live up there in the cold? Why don't you live down here in the sunshine belt? Life here is much easier."

"I like it up there. I like snow. I like seasons. I don't want life to be too easy."

"You're crazy, you know that? Okay, so what have you actually told me? That poets are too busy thinking about higher things to have to worry about money?"

"Oh, Christ! Poets worry about money all the time. They just don't think it's the most important thing in the world." I'm sick of this conversation. Can you ever really explain the creative urge?

"Maybe," I tell him, "I write poems for the same reason you make money. It gives me some sense of having control over what might otherwise seem a senseless life. It makes me feel less passive, less a victim. It gives me a tiny sense of power." I am undone. "Damn it," I say, "I don't know what it means."

"If I may say so," he says softly, "money gives me a large sense of power. It's real. It is power."

I turn my hands palm up on the table, a gesture of surrender, and groan. "I write poems," I tell Arty Tannenbaum, "because that's what I do."

"You're not eating," he says after a moment. "You mad at me? Don't be mad at me." He grins engagingly, happy to have won. "You know what? You and me are gonna be friends."

SIXTEEN (then)

"Who's unhappy?"

"You just said you were unhappy."

"I said I wasn't happy. I'm not unhappy, either."

"Yeah."

The telephone crackled. Belle's cat must have chewed the wires again; her phone often sounded as though it lay at the bottom of an ocean or in the baggage compartment of an airplane. But Ann knew it was on the kitchen wall just beside the bay of half-shuttered windows. Belle would be sitting at the kitchen table with a pencil in her hand, yesterday's Times spread out before her, looking out at the birch tree they had planted and at the kids on the block gathered under the tree with their pails and shovels and kitchen spoons, digging beneath the dog turds at the poor sad soil in which the tree was working so hard to put down serious roots. The children would be noisy and messy and after a while, when Belle went out to shoo them away, they would hurl incredibly precocious obscenities at her. The neighborhood was changing.

"Yesterday," Ann said. "God, it was a bad day! One of those really lo-o-ong days . . ."

She'd gone to her studio after breakfast, when the kids had left for school. Two years earlier when Jed had begun school, she had made the smallest bedroom, which sometimes doubled as a guest room, into a studio. She, too, had gone to school, a writing workshop at NYU, in order to get the feedback she felt she needed to keep herself serious, at least in the beginning. And also to get herself out of Sparrow Fart Lane and back into the real world.

It was nearly a dozen years since she'd stopped writing.

She closed the studio door and sat at the desk, waiting for words. The room was at the back of the house, the desk overlooking the garden, the brook, the woods beyond. She stared out, trying not to think about the garden. Nature. A firefly had gotten into the bedroom last night. Herbie was asleep but she had stayed up reading. When she put out the light, she saw, with the same tingle of excitement and wonder she remembered feeling as a small child, the brief intermittent flashing of the firefly. She lay waiting for the next light, trying to guess where it would appear, marveling at how tiny patches of darkness were fleetingly illuminated by this odd, bumbling insect. Firefly as metaphor. A poem?

She looked up firefly in her Library of the Natural Sciences and read that "the male flies about signaling while the female remains perched on low plants in the meadow. When the female sees the male's signal, she responds with a well- timed flash slightly weaker than his. In giving her response, the female twists her abdomen to throw her light in the direction of the male. Her response-flash excites the male, and he descends toward her, constantly flashing his signal. Presently, he meets the maiden pyralis; they introduce themselves formally, and in due course become the parents of next year's crop of Photinus pyralis."

It was practically a poem already, a found poem.

She thought of the ways in which creatures of the earth chose to speak to their kind, to invite them to love, and the way of the firefly seemed particularly charming. She thought herself into a firefly circling lazily in the summer night, a male. How soft the fragrant air. Light of my life, my loinfire burns for thee. Oh maiden in the summer grass below, see me circling aloft, signaling my lust, on off, on off, and when you catch my burning backward glance, respond. Turn and gleam your timid lamp at me. Then I, enflamed . . .

The house was too quiet.

Let others speak their love in song or rasp, croak, bellow, sigh or gasp. Or scent their message borne on air to lovers' noses/ invisible bouquets/ a heat of summer roses.

Something was wrong.

How Victorian, the female lolling below with her more modest light, earthbound and passive, while those rakish showoffs in the sky above flashed and flashed, waiting to be noticed, to be invited.

Why was it too quiet? Herbie was gone, the children were gone. There were only herself and the new houseworker. Penny. Penny was too quiet. Penny ought to be making sounds. They had hired her on Monday, hope springing eternal.

The star's mirror is my way. I call upon oxygen, luciferase, luciferin, and command of my derrière a beacon through which, begging your pardon, my love may shine.

Penny was smart, a tall, copper-colored woman with freckles and orangey-black hair braided around her head. Part black, part Indian, she'd said, obviously proud of the Indian part.

As if on cue, there was a horrendous crash from below. Ann flew downstairs into the kitchen. Penny was sprawled on the floor, half-sitting, her legs spread before her like open scissor blades. Shards of breakfast dishes lay scattered across the floor, broken shells on a beach in the aftermath of a storm.

"Penny!" Ann gasped. "What happened?"

Penny, her eyes glazed, stared straight ahead.

"Are you hurt? I'll call a doctor. Can you get up?"

"No docker," Penny mumbled. "Okay in a minute."

"Let me help you up." For some reason, it was important to get her up off the floor. Penny pushed her away.

"Doan wanna get up," she said, alcohol fumes filling the air. Ann sat down on a kitchen chair.

"Touch dizziness," Penny said.

"Can I get you something? A glass of water?"

"No water."

"I'll help you to your room. You should be in bed."

"Perfeckly okay right here."

"Better in bed."

"Wazza matter with right here, Miz Fuckface?"

"Oh shit," Ann said.

"Bet you think I'm drunk, Miz Whitey Fuckface. No such of a thing. Neurological episode. Comes on from hate. Doan wanna wash your floors."

"Don't wash my floors."

"Why should I, Miz Jewshit? How come you doan wash my floors?"

"Stop calling me names, Penny. Life is unfair. You applied for this job."

"Doan want this fuckin job." She tilted and slumped further toward the floor. "I'm better'n any fuckin Jewass any day inna week," she said, and fell asleep. Ann watched her for a while, wondering what to do. Nothing. Let her sleep it off. But it was no longer possible to go up to her ivory tower and write about the love life of fireflies.

"So much hate," Ann said to Belle. "She was there for three hours. I cleaned the bedrooms and ran two washes. When she came to, she didn't remember a thing. The perfect lady. Apologized for the dishes. Said she sometimes had these neurological episodes, nothing serious, brought on by the colliding of her bloods."

"The what?"

"Said she was one hundred percent Seminole Indian on her mother's side and the Indian blood was at war with her other blood, like when the body tries to reject a foreign part, and that sometimes it made her black out, you should pardon the expression, and fall down."

"Anti-white. Anti-black. Anti-Semitic."

"When I told her to pack up and leave, she refused to go. Started calling me Miz Jew Fuckface again when I told her I wouldn't give her two weeks' pay. She'd worked a day and a half."

She sat down on the floor again, folded her arms across her breast and refused to budge, not without one hundred dollars in her pocket.

"By then I was beginning to be frightened," Ann said. "I went upstairs to the bedroom, locked the door, and called the police. I think it was the first time I was glad to be a tax-payer. They were wonderful. Very patient and gentle with Penny, but firm. I paid her a week's salary and when she threw it on the floor, the police picked it up and tucked it in her pocket and took her to her room and got her packed, then drove her to the station and put her on a train."

With the departure of the last of the au pair girls nearly a year ago, a beautiful Swede who left after several months to abort the fetus she'd acquired instead of the English she'd come for, Ann had called it quits. No more "help." What a relief not to have to cope with the problems of strangers! What a relief not to have to cope with her own guilt!

"The house is too big," Herbie argued. "You can't do it all yourself and still expect to spend any decent time writing."

But she had prevailed. So what if the house was messy, meals less than gourmet, and the laundry, which she began sending out, came back imperfectly ironed and with an occasional button or sock missing. It was a small price to pay for the time she needed. But Herbie minded. You had only to compare his closet and drawers with hers to know which of them was the neat one. She often told him that he'd have made someone the perfect compulsive housewife, that it was too bad he'd been born a husband. He insisted that somewhere out there the perfect live-in houseworker waited for them to find her and he was going to do it.

Penny was the fourth in the weeks since Ann had succumbed.

"When she was gone," Ann said, "I found the empty bottle in her room. Johnny Walker Black. We had two bottles left over from Christmas there among the Red."

"Considering her bloods, you'd think she'd have chosen the Red."

"Then I found the top drawer of the bureau in her room filled with used sanitary napkins."

"That explains it. She was having her period."

"I think that was the most frightening thing of all. It seemed so violent, all that hatred. In my own house."

"You can always sell the house and move."

They both laughed. Ann had done it twice. They had sold the last house because late one night she'd awakened hungry and gone downstairs for something to eat. When she switched on the light at the bottom of the stairs, she found herself face to face with a small black animal that stood, frozen, in the middle of the living room. They stared into each other's eyes for what could only have been a split second but seemed much longer, and then the creature scampered into and up the fireplace.

"It was a rat," she told Herbie.

"Probably a squirrel."

"A rat. It had a mean little face and beady eyes. Squirrels sleep at night. I don't care what it was. What was it doing in our living room?"

"This is the country."

"It's a lousy suburb. If at least it were the country."

"We'll screen the top of the chimney."

"It's too late. The house is ruined."

She'd found this house, more rooms, less charm, brand new, still smelling of plaster, and there was no way, with the storms and screens installed, that anything larger than a firefly could get in except by ringing the doorbell first.

"Since I was already in such a lousy mood," Ann told Belle, "I figured I might as well pay bills and do the bank statement. Among the bills was one from Herbie's favorite haberdasher on Madison Avenue for a few items he'd picked up. Over $600 worth."

"He's a businessman," Belle said. Belle always made excuses for everyone else. "He has to look successful."

"Underwear? Pajamas?"

Sometimes, to calm herself, Ann would go into Jed's room and watch his hamster running on its wheel. The hamster was onto something. It was as good a life as most, the treadmill, and it kept you from getting fat and lazy.

"Then I decided to do the bank statement to see if there was enough money to cover everything. There was almost nothing. I couldn't believe it because by my reckoning there should have been a pretty decent balance."

It was she who paid the bills and made deposits. Herbie gave her the stubs from his pocket checkbook every week so that she could keep the balance current.

"I went over and over it and then I saw a $4500 debit on the statement that I couldn't account for. I called the bank to tell them they'd made an error and they checked and said no, the debit was for a bank collection, the first monthly payment against a loan they'd made to Herbie. I said there had to be some mistake, but I knew there wasn't. I asked how many monthly payments there were going to be and they said thirty."

"Oy!"

"My sentiments exactly. I couldn't even call Herbie to ask what it was about. I knew he'd tell me some lie. I just sat and stared at the wall and wondered how I could have been living with this man for eighteen years in what I believed was reasonable intimacy, a man who has $135,000 worth of something in his life that I know nothing about, something he's neglected to mention. There's no way we can pay off that debt for the next two and half years, not without selling the house and living in a cave, eating roots."

"What was it?"

"Is. One of his sure-fire schemes. Something he's been working on for months with this character he thinks is a genius, a little pink and white rabbit of a swindler with the

Later, she went upstairs and looked in his drawers and counted and it was another lie. It was all there. She sat in the bathtub in steaming water and wept.

Belle sighed. "So what else is new?" she asked.

"My firefly poem," Ann said. "I think I finished it this morning. Maybe."

SEVENTEEN (Now)

"Why do you live way up there in freezing New Hampshire?" Artie asks. "Why'd you leave New York City?"

"Because of the bank," I tell him. "I fell in love with it. It's a long story."

"Tell me while we're dancing. Can you Mamba?"

"No."

"Come on. Now that you've taught me all about poetry, I'll teach you the Mamba and meanwhile you can tell me about the bank."

He pulls me onto the dance floor.

"One two three, one two three."

"That's all?"

"Practically. Start with that. One two three. What about the bank?"

"When I lived in New York," I say, watching my feet, "I used a branch of a bank that thought of itself as friendly. For six years, I went into that bank about three times a week. What's that, about 950 visits?"

"You're quicker with figures than with your feet."

"I'd stand in a long line, between ropes, as though I was waiting to see a terrific movie instead of making a deposit. When I finally got to the teller's window, some sour underpaid person who never looked up took my check and my I.D. card. The card had my signature and my account number. I had a savings account and a checking account in this bank and there was always a reasonable balance in both. I was never overdrawn."

"Your left foot now. It's simple. After the right foot, the left."

"Still, if God forbid I should one day find myself without the I.D. card, I couldn't have cashed a check. The teller wouldn't have known what to tell the machine so that the machine could search its memory and give the teller permission to let me have my money. The teller not only didn't know me, he never even saw me. He was an automaton and I was, too --- a customer robot who handed over a piece of plastic to a teller robot who stuck it in a machine and pushed some buttons. And even that machine was just a middle-machine for the major machine. Finally, the teller would get the okay from the machine and he'd count out the money and he'd hand it to me and say next."

"Now do it in reverse. Like this."

"It was only a question of time before the teller would go, too, and it would be only me, my plastic card, and the machine, which is better, really. You don't expect a machine to look up and recognize you, maybe even smile. And it's more polite. But then, when it was still tellers, I once had a check to deposit, a $50,000 check. It wasn't really mine; it was some sort of transaction between my father and me, but I had to deposit it to my account before giving him back my own check for that amount."

"Good. Keep doing that."

"I couldn't wait to go to the bank to deposit that check, to pass it to the teller and see the expression on his face when he looked at it. There would have to be some tiny reaction to it, surprise, awe, respect. It seemed such an enormous amount of money to me. I thought surely the teller would have to look at me then, even if it was just one fleeting, slightly curious look."

"Did he?"

"No. Nothing. It could have been a check for $5. How I hated that bank!"

"Move your hips a little more. Like this."

"That summer I rented a cottage in the woods in a little resort town on a lake in New Hampshire, north of where I live now. There was a big supermarket a few miles away where, the day I moved in, I went to stock up. I love supermarkets. This one was privately owned, not part of a huge chain. But it was vast. It had everything, even bagels in the freezer."

"That's unusual?"

"In New Hampshire? Anyhow, I'd just arrived and I needed everything, all the basics. There was a big freezer compartment in the refrigerator in the cottage, so I figured I could market for at least a week, since I was there to work, not to market. I began loading up my cart. I had some cash and traveler's checks and a check for a couple of thousand dollars that I meant to deposit somewhere to open a checking account for the summer. In the produce section between the potatoes and onions there was an open door and I looked inside and lo, there was a bank, a dear little bank the size of a country kitchen. Right in the market. It was there mainly for the drive-in window that opened onto the parking lot."

"You can stop dancing now. The band isn't playing any more." Still holding onto my hand, he leads me back to the table. "You tell a long story," he says.

"I know. This one is endless. Do you want me to stop?"

"No. I'm, what's the word, transfixed."

"So I parked my cart next to the onions and went inside and said I wanted to open an account. They filled out a card and I gave them my check and they gave me some temporary blank checks. I asked when I could start drawing on the account and they said right away. I pointed out that my check was on an out-of-town bank and they said that was okay. I asked what the checking charge was and they told me there wasn't any, so I asked what is the minimum balance and they said just leave, you know, a couple of dollars in the account. I thanked them and left but I had a peculiar feeling that there must be something wrong with that bank."

"Hey, there's a Cha Cha. C'mon."

"I went back to my cart and finished marketing," I continue, following him back to the dance floor, where I fall into his embrace. He's a strong leader. "It was a busy market for such a small town. They did a lot of business with vacationers, the lake in summer, skiing in winter. When I'd filled the basket so full there wasn't room for one more thing, I got on one of the checkout lines. There were six and, unlike New York supermarkets, all of them were manned. Well, actually, womanned."

"That's not the Cha Cha. You're still doing the Mamba."

"I don't know the Cha Cha. I only know the Mamba."

"Watch me."

"A lot of people, I noticed, were charging their groceries so I thought I'd see about opening a charge account, too, for future visits. I asked the clerk about it when my turn came and she called over the manager who, I later learned, was also the owner. He whipped out a yellow card, asked my name, and printed it on top and then he asked for my mailing address. I told him General Delivery, George's Mills, and he wrote that down and handed the card to the clerk and smiled and told me to have a good summer and when the checker had it all added up it came to over eighty-five dollars and, without even asking, she put it on the charge card!"

"Wrong! You're doing a tango."

"Nonsense. I don't know how to tango."

"That is definitely a tango."

"Are you listening to my story?"

"I haven't missed a word."

"Then you understand? They'd never seen me before. They had no way of knowing that they'd ever see me again. They didn't have a real address for me. And they let me walk out of there with all those groceries!"

"I don't think you like to dance."

"What I really like is to dance alone. I feel private about social dancing. It seems so personal."

"All right, we'll sit down. Maybe then you'll get to the end of this story."

"I told you it was long."

"It's okay. I love stories about money."

"Well, by the time I left that market, I knew there was not only something wrong with the bank but the same thing was wrong with the market. Maybe the town, too. Maybe the whole state. But I couldn't put my finger on exactly what it was. I just felt vaguely uneasy. I drove back to the cottage and began unloading the groceries. My cat was asleep in a patch of sunlight on the big screened porch, and she opened one eye when I got back and then she closed it again. You'd have thought we'd been living there forever instead of about eighteen hours. I wondered if the cat felt safe because she trusted me, and then I realized that that was what was strange about the market and the bank. They trusted me. It couldn't have been anything personal. They must have trusted everyone."

"Ha! Try trusting in New York. Or even here."

"But if they trusted everyone, it must have meant that everyone was trustworthy. Did it mean that people were trusted because they were trustworthy, or the other way around? Was it cause and effect, and in which order? I finally understood that both were necessary simultaneously, that the condition that prevailed there arose out of the kind of innocence and purity that must have predated original sin. It was original innocence. Vis-a-vis money, I was back in the Garden of Eden."

"Now they're playing a tango. Want to try it?"

"Can't you sit still for one minute?"

"But that's not the bank you fell in love with, is it? We're not even up to that, are we?"

"I transferred my affection to the bank where I live now when I discovered that it was exactly the same as the little bank up north, except that it's much larger and has a lovely waterfall out back."

He orders a fresh drink for me. He's barely touched his own.

"My love was cemented," I say, "one bitterly cold day when I woke to find that there was no heat."

Angie lay in a heap on the sofa where she'd passed out some time during the night. I piled blankets on top of her.

shrewdest eyes you ever saw, one of those glib phonies any-one in the world except Herbie could see through."

"He's such a sophisticated man," Belle said. "It's hard to understand."

"His dream is one perfect coup, and he's so eager for it that he'll convince himself of anything. His fantasies make him euphoric. He's like a hippo wallowing in mud. He calls me 'Oh ye of little faith.' Says this is the one, that by next month the entire loan will be paid off. Says there's a big backer excited about it. Says it's some kind of dandy supermarket coupon scheme that positively can't miss."

"Could it be true, do you think?"

"What difference does it make what I think?"

"Do you think he thinks it's true?"

"Oh, absolutely."

"Does he make it all up?"

"No, just the parts that don't fit. When I spot the loopholes and bring them to his attention, I can actually see him inventing the little answers that pick up the dropped stitches, and then I watch him believing himself. By the time he's finished, he's happy and I'm a wreck, in a helpless rage. Last night, when he'd explained it all, his eyes were glowing. He'd turned this catastrophe into his shining triumph, swept us out of bankruptcy and onto the ballroom floor where we swooned into a marvelous waltz while the violins played and the waiters in white gloves brought on the shmerz."

"Schlag. Shmerz is pain."

He stood there smiling brilliantly, victorious, waiting for her to throw her arms around him, her hero, her dauntless lover. Instead, she showed him the underwear bill.

"Oh that," he said. "I returned half of it. They'll be sending a credit."

"The oil tank had run dry," I tell Artie.

Angie had driven up the previous night to say, "It's all right, you can come home now." When she had seen the tenants moving out of the city apartment adjoining ours, she had immediately rented it and arranged with the landlord to break through a closet wall to make one apartment out of the two. "We've been too crowded," she said. "That's why it's been so hard. We haven't had enough space."

"I phoned the oil company and they were very apologetic," I tell Artie. "Someone had goofed, but unfortunately the driver was already out and they didn't know if they could contact him before late afternoon."

"That's not why," I said. "I can't come back."

"I'm so lonely without you. Please, darling."

"I'm lonely, too," I said. "But it won't work. We're hurting each other too much."

"It was no great tragedy because I was going out back to my studio to work and that's heated by electricity, so I put on my coat and boots, picked up the cat, and carried her to the studio and settled down to work."

"You take your cat to work?"

"I can't write without a cat. They sit on your finished pages and purr. Or yawn. Or sleep. They're very calming."

"I've stopped drinking," Angie said. "Really, this time."

"I'd been working for about an hour when the typewriter suddenly quit. I jiggled it and fooled with the plug and checked the fuse box and couldn't find anything wrong, so I settled down to read."

Angie would sleep for a long time. God knew when she finally collapsed into sleep. Even in the cold, the air reeked of booze.

"Soon, I noticed that I was shivering. I looked at the thermostat and the heat was way down. The electricity had gone off. I put on my coat and boots and went back to the house to call the power company. The wires were down because of ice. The electricity was out all over the neighborhood. They were working on it. I put on an extra sweater and decided to make a huge fire in the fireplace."

Angie stirred and, in a small, muffled voice, said, "I'm cold."

"Nothing's working," I told her. "I'm going to make a fire in the studio. When I get it going you can finish sleeping on the cot there." But Angie was already asleep.

"Then I remembered that I'd used the last of the wood in the studio and I'd have to carry some over from the basement in the house, where it's stored. I started down the basement steps but it was too dark for me to see. There was a flashlight in the car. I put on my boots and coat and went out to the car to get it, then made a couple of trips lugging wood to the studio. When I began to lay the fire, I discovered that there was no newspaper in the studio. Back to the house."

Angie was sitting up, wrapped in blankets, with a mug of coffee and an unlit cigarette. She looked small and pale and sick. I wanted to take her in my arms and hold her and tell her everything would be all right, but I didn't. Because it wouldn't.

"I can't find any matches," Angie said.

"I hunted, but there wasn't a match in the house," I tell Artie. "I went through every drawer, all my pockets, the bottoms of handbags. It never would have happened if I hadn't quit smoking. That was the first time I quit, and it didn't last too long. So by then I was feeling paranoid, to say nothing of exhausted from all that running back and forth, pulling boots on and off, but I was simply going to have to go to town for matches. I was sure the car wouldn't start, but for a wonder it did. As I was driving, it occurred to me that it was Friday and the markets would be busy. I could avoid the checkout lines if I went to the bank for matches."

"The bank?"

"It's a full service bank," I say, and giggle. "On the counter next to each teller's window is a lovely large glass bowl filled, not with flowers or tossed salad, but with wide double matchbooks advertising the bank. I parked the car and as I was climbing the steps to the bank, I felt silly about just going in and grabbing a handful of matches and leaving. So I did a stupid little lying charade: rummaged in my coat pockets, unbuttoned my coat and reached into my pants pockets, trying to make my face look increasingly concerned and chagrined. Then I grimaced, took the matches, and turned to leave. All the while, though, I felt so dopey and self-conscious, embarrassed by my behavior, because who did I think was paying any attention to me, who would care? But as I turned to leave, a woman, not even a teller but someone sitting at a desk behind the tellers, got up and came forward, smiling, and asked me if I'd lost anything. I said I'd forgotten my checkbook and I'd come back later. 'No need, Mrs. Becker,' she said. She knew my name! She whipped out a blank check and slid it toward me with one hand, grabbing a fistful of bills with the other. 'How much do you want?' 'I don't know my account number,' I said, lamely, because I knew there would be no stopping her. 'That's all right,' she said, 'I'll look it up.' I left with the matches and $40 that she had forced on me. When I got home, the electricity was working and the oilman was filling the tank."

Angie was at the door in her coat.

"I'm going," she said. "I hope I can stand it."

"Me too," I said. "I'll always love you."

I watched Angie walk away to her car. The back of her neck. She drove off and I cried and cried. It was the last time I saw her.

"That's the reason I love my bank," I tell Artie. "And it's one of the reasons I live way up there in the frozen north."

EIGHTEEN (then)

At The Colony, the words began to come. Sometimes they were upside down, sometimes slightly askew, but she was seeing the world fresh, the way it was when she was a child and sometimes free, when everything was new and discrete, unconnected to other things and blurred by them, in that time of long hours before the blinkers of habit and judgment and self-censorship. Her mind ticked. Nothing was unimportant or beneath notice; everything was new and hectic with excitement. A page turned and she was no longer the writer; she was part of the story, alive in it. She was in love with life, with this odd, mysterious place, with everyone there, with her words, with herself. She was ready, she felt, for anything.

The words came. They came willy-nilly, making that mysterious leap from what the senses have brought to the mind, the heart, the center of feeling and knowing, there to be sorted and classified, then sent forth again, through the fingers onto the page where the eye receives them in this new order and form, and the mind, surprised, thinks: did I say that? did I know that? ah, so that's how it was! How remarkable this making concrete what was ephemeral and yet making it concrete in this ephemeral way. Language, such an arbitrary stew of symbols, each standing for an approximation of something, the window, salt, the end of a life.

Tree. Tree alone says something, conjuring up an image, but is it an oak, a cedar, how does it smell, is it tall, is it young, is it in leaf, are its leaves turning, falling, greening? So much depends on the good faith between the sender and the receiver, and on their devotion: the sender to choose well, the receiver to listen with care. Tree was enough if she needed it for the dog to lift its leg against, but if she needed it for the cold moon to shine through its bare twisted branches, then she had decided on winter, on deciduous, on ancient, and perhaps on a mood, a state of mind.

Even though the words came all day, when they gathered for dinner at night, they talked and talked. After dinner, too. Angie wouldn't arrive for another week. Ann had not yet fallen in love.

"I feel that I was chosen, that I am merely a vessel," Santha said. She was a novelist, better known outside her country than in it. "Like a bulb, an electric bulb through which the light may shine."

Santha was Indian, a Hindu, and Ann knew little of Eastern philosophy. She had no idea if what Santha believed relieved her of responsibility or demanded more of it. Or was responsibility, as Ann conceived it, a western notion?

They were discussing "the process," and Ann thought about herself, and the way in which she must first empty her mind in order for the thoughts, and the words for the thoughts, to well up. If Santha was a light bulb, then she, Ann, was some kind of plumbing.

She didn't want to be either.

"It's *my* experience," she insisted. "Out of *my* life. In *my* voice." Oh, America! "Even when I invent it, it's my invention." She was suddenly so possessive of it, and so unwilling to be passive, to be merely a vehicle. "What else is the self?"

Santha smiled. "Never the twain," she said in her sweet lilting voice. But it wasn't true. Half the people at the table meditated twice a day and would eat nothing but vegetables. Half the children of Ann's friends, if they weren't wearing saffron *shmattas* and begging in the streets, were in ashrams or in retreat, unlearning all their basic assumptions, coming home only briefly to demonstrate how patient and wise and superior they were to their psychotherapist mothers and lawyer fathers who had bartered their souls for a second car and a second home full of major and minor appliances, and who were so busy catering to their egos.

"So you do it because it's already there in the ether waiting for you to transmit it?" she said. "Because it's chosen you?"

"Why do you do it?"

Order. Control. Love. To discover who she was, what she thought. "The world --- the shadow of the soul, or other me, lies wide around. Its attractions are the key which unlock my thoughts and make me acquainted with myself. I run eagerly (now I do) into this resounding tumult. I grasp the hands of those next to me, and take my place in the ring to suffer and to work, taught by an instinct that so shall the dumb abyss be vocal with speech." --- Emerson.

She felt that she had changed her life, that she had come so much further than the two hundred odd miles she'd driven only a few weeks ago. And how hard it was to do! Who was that frail, frightened creature whose hands shook so that she could hardly turn the key in the ignition?

"Take it easy," Herbie said, leaning into the window to give her a last goodbye kiss, this time on the cheek, a friend's kiss. "Relax. We're not even going to miss you. Enjoy it."

She touched the gas pedal and the motor began to hum. It was a dandy little car, quick and eager, and she loved the look of it, trim and purposeful and as blue as the sky of this early summer day. It was her car, the first that wasn't a station wagon, that didn't tell her by its practical roominess what her duties were, where her usefulness lay.

"It's a perfect day for a drive," Herbie said, as though she were off on a lark and would be back in time for dinner. "Go already! I can't stand long goodbyes."

But still she idled there in the driveway with her trembling sweaty hands, her stomach a block of ice. Her limbs had lost their bones; they would never be able to do what they must to take her the distance she had to travel. She simply couldn't do it! She cast wildly about, insanely hoping for one of the boys to materialize with a non-negotiable reason why she mustn't go. But the boys had said their goodbyes and gone off, Jed in the yellow minibus that took him to day camp, Nick on his bike to the baseball field. Fanny, however, still stood in the doorway, waving and smiling her beautiful smile, good, motherly Fanny, gentle and loving, adored by them all, who had finally, magically materialized. "Go!" she told herself, waving back, ashamed now not to go. She released the brake.

"I'll call tonight," she told Herbie, easing the car out of the driveway, trying to smile, knowing by the tightness she felt in the muscles of her face that her fear showed. Dr. Kantfogel, to whom she still sometimes ran with a crisis, had said, beaming with pride, not in her but in his own success, "Of course you can do it, of course you'll go," and given her a prescription for a tranquilizer. She'd taken one that morning. If this was how she felt with it, she couldn't imagine the quivering reed she'd have been without it. "It comes with the doing," Kantfogel had assured her. "That's the only way the pattern breaks. You're really beginning now. It will get easier, I promise you."

She turned the corner of Red Maple Lane, out of sight of the house. Her street, her house, her people, her books and clothes. If anyone had ever told her that her center would one day be there, on a street named Red Maple Lane!

In spite of her melting limbs, her stomach cramps, the tremendous effort it took to hold herself together, she somehow got the car onto the parkway and almost to the cutoff for the Thruway. One step at a time, the way she'd taken most of her life. Think about something else, she told herself, take stock. A suburban wife, a loving, handsome husband, two gorgeous kids, a large dog, who could ask for anything more? Wife, mother, daughter; mother, daughter, wife. Think about all the socks you won't have to roll into balls in the next two months. Two months! No planning what to have for dinner, no shopping lists, no marketing, no cooking, no paying bills or balancing the checkbook (Herbie would have to do it, God help them all), no phone calls with friends to arrange evenings, or weekend visits with parents; no nagging Nick to do his homework, or taking Jed for piano lessons, to the pediatrician, to the dentist, to his friend Bobbie's house; no P.T.A. meetings or bringing the car in to have the oil changed, or Chump, the big sweet dumb Newfoundland, to the vet for shots.

If she died, all these things would somehow get done without her. They would manage.

But she hadn't died. She was driving to a place where she'd never been, and into two months of time that would be entirely her own, to be filled with what? Words, words, work. Her work. She had been invited. It was an honor. There would be people there, other writers, artists, real ones.

They would know at once that she was a fraud. Don't think about it.

She was crossing the Tappan Zee Bridge. Its construction was begun the summer she and Herbie were still living in the castle with her parents, the summer of her breakdown. Often during the day they could hear the distant pounding of pile drivers. There had been some controversy about the location of the bridge; why there at the river's widest point? Did they need a bridge exactly there? Later, when it was built, she liked to think that the site had been chosen precisely because it was the least practical, that the decision hadn't been that of a consortium of engineers, politicians, unions, but as the vision of some romantic, a dreamer, who had wanted this long and graceful span with its generous views up and down as well as across the beautiful Hudson River. At the far shore, white wings of sailboats scudded in small flocks, like cabbage butterflies, mirroring the soft puffs of clouds that moved lazily across the sky.

When she stopped not long afterward at the toll booth for her ticket, it occurred to her that she was going to be trapped on the Thruway; how many miles to the next exit? and felt the familiar panic resurgent. She fought it down. You can do it, she told herself, daughter, wife, mother, friend, ex-patient. You're a big girl, now, you have your own key.

But she was driving away from all the roles, from the doors the key opened. No wonder she was frightened, close to panic, her stomach knotted again in pain. She was leaving all her familiar selves. Who then would she be? Still, even away from them, they would define her. Wasn't she still what she had been, that person?

And then it came clear. She was going to a place where she was known, where she mattered, only as herself, this new self she had at last, tentatively, slowly begun to be, this separate self. It was because of the few things she had published that she had been invited to spend this time working among other poets, writers, painters, composers. Other, that was the key word. If there were others, she was one of them. One.

It was the first time. She would be forty on her next birthday, and it was the first time in her life that she was doing something that was just for herself, her own. The first time that she would be responsible only to herself. She began to cry. She had never really known, not this deep gut knowing, how entirely her sense of herself had depended on others, their needs of her, hers of them. It had taken forty years for her to be able to take this first shaky, timid, outrageously bold step.

She was no longer weeping. She looked at the odometer and reckoned that she was about midway there. She began to sing.

It must have been then that she became I, when I sang at the top of her lungs with the joy of hearing my own voice, off-key though it was, with the joy of the lovely day, with the joy of feeling my past life fly further behind and the joy of the unknown future I was flying to meet. It was my future. Whatever it held, it would be my own. I'm ready for it. The fear is gone. There is only this freedom, this joy.

NINETEEN (Now)

"How about we make love?" Artie asks, looking coy. He's careful with me, refined.

"Maybe later," I say, as though we're an old married couple. We haven't yet made love, and I'm not sure I want to. The last time I saw him, he kissed me goodnight.

"You're so romantic," he says.

"Well, I'm starving, aren't you?" Breakfast was hours ago and we've had nothing since but all this fresh air. But it's a stupid question. I doubt if this man is ever hungry. Passing the big wooden ice chest where a fish or two still sound an occasional thump, dying at length, I go to the galley. Obviously, no one has ever cooked here, it's so clean, so virginal, so undisturbed. All forty feet of the Princess Doris II are immaculate, shipshape. When Artie isn't using it, the yacht lies in a marina where, like Doris's grave, it receives perpetual care. And when Artie is using it, he's constantly fussing with it. He's now throwing the remnants of the bait overboard for the screaming gulls that swoop to retrieve it before it hits the water. Next, he will dismantle the rods. We aren't going to fish any more. We've already caught more fish than we can possibly use, although it's only a little past noon.

"I know plenty of widows very happy to get a nice fresh fish," Artie says, when I ask what we're going to do with our catch. "They put them in the freezer compartment and then invite me over to dinner. Surprise, they say, it's your own fish. In exchange for eating my own fish, I'm supposed to ask them to marry me."

I laugh. "The fish as bait to catch a larger fish," I say.

"But the larger fish wants to catch you," he says.

I ignore this, fervently hoping it's not a preamble to anything serious. The galley's neatness oppresses me. It does my heart good to clutter it up with the stuff I picked up at the Royal early this morning, sandwiches and mustard and pickles and coleslaw and beer. "Corned beef? Turkey? Roast beef? Tongue?" I call. "Half of each?"

"It doesn't matter."

"Is there anything you don't like? I mean, is there anything you do like?"

"Okay, half a turkey, to start."

I bring it all out on a tray.

"Jesus," he says, looking at it, "there's only you and me here."

It's another perfect blue and golden day. The monotony of it. Nothing but perfect days. White gulls hover, echoing the white puffs of clouds that sit low on the horizon, deepening the blue of the sky. The greener blue of the calm sea laps softly against the side of the boat as it rocks gently at anchor. I'd give anything for the sky to darken, for a storm to blow up. I sit, not on one of the captain's chairs in the stern, but on the deck itself, my face turned toward the sun, breathing the pure air that's so balmy one could spoon it like honey.

"This is living," I sigh, chewing corned beef.

"Like I said. You really should move down here." Finished dismantling and stowing away the fishing gear, he pulls off his knit shirt with the little polo player on the pocket, carefully folds it across the back of a chair, and comes and sprawls beside me. He has the spare, long-muscled body of a swimmer, brown and lean and graceful. Though my mouth is full of corned beef, he leans across to kiss me, his tongue moving lightly across my mouth. Then he pulls back and looks at me slyly.

"You had mustard on your mouth is the only reason I did that," he says, grinning, reaching for half a turkey sandwich.

"You're a neat and fussy man," I say. "It must be all those years making paper napkins."

He laughs. "I'm also a lovable man. You'll see."

Do I want to make love with him? I feel no compelling urge, but the idea doesn't repel me, either. Beginnings.

When we realized we'd fallen in love, Angie and I were astonished, we were so unlike anyone either of us had expected. Astonished and euphoric, madly, wildly happy. Oh, the excitement, the breadth and depth and latitude of it. That first time, we made love all night long, one candle burning, its small fluttery light in the huge room, Angie's room, and the rain falling softly into the treetops that waved like feathery ghosts outside the windows. The candlelight fluttery like my heart when I knew we were going to make love, when I knew there was no way not to.

Yes, I'll make love with Artie, but more out of boredom. And a little curiosity. I've been celibate for more than a year. It's been much longer than that since I've made love with a man. I wonder how it will feel and if my body still works. I know I could never fall in love with Artie, but I'm comfortable with him. And it's been such a sweetly sensual day.

"I don't know if I'll know how," I said

"You'll know how," Angie said, smiling, and we be-gan, through the long, wonderful night, to discover each other, to discover ourselves.

"All right," I say, pushing away the tray, as I would have pushed away all memory of Angie if I could. Obsession is sickness, I tell myself, licking my fingers. "Let's try it."

He stares at me. "You've hardly eaten a thing. You haven't even finished half a sandwich." Nonetheless, he swivels to meet me, puts his arms around me and covers my mouth with his. Slowly, for a long time, behind closed eyes, we are inside each other's mouths. Unlike Angie, Artie neither smokes nor drinks and, because of his eating habits, I'm sure he's never dyspeptic. He tastes faintly of Russian dressing, nothing else. He undoes my shirt and his hands begin to move over me. I try not to think, to give myself over to pure sensation, to exist only in my nerve endings. He's a skilled lover, experienced and considerate and unhurried, and for a while I'm aware of that, and of the hardness of his body, the rough texture and smell of his skin, the curling graying hair of his chest. His body doesn't melt and flow and fit into mine. Instead, I feel his bones, his angularity, the heat of him. But I find myself responding. In a way, although his lovemaking is gentle, we've become antagonists, even though we are striving for the same thing. At some point, I stop cataloguing differences and become all body, except for one small corner of my mind where there are blue lights and white lights and a silent voice that says yes that, don't stop doing that, yes good, and now and now. Then, while he is deep inside me, he stops moving and says something. I open my eyes and look up at him. His head is dark against the sky.

"Who's your man?" he says. His eyes are burning, his face is so serious it's almost angry. "Who's your man?" I can tell it's something he always says, has always said, at this moment of near-triumph. He will go on saying it until I tell him what he wants to hear. Say uncle. Is that what he needs to reach orgasm? I can't believe it. "Come on, who's your man?" I'm supposed to be writhing, gasping, "Oh you, Artie, you're my man, oh God! My lover, my man. Please, Artie, oh please." For one desperate moment, I consider indulging him, such a small and silly thing, but I can't get my mouth around the words. Instead, I can't help it, I laugh.

"Shut up, Artie," I say, and feel him begin to go soft inside me. He looks puzzled, and then we resume, trying to take up where we left off. Slowly, slowly, though the inevitability is lost, and the anonymity, and the pure pleasure, and what we're doing is with gritted teeth, hard work, we get back to where we were. In a little while, or perhaps it's a long while, I manage to shut out all thought and go down to that deep solitary place. My coming releases him, and together, groaning, we shudder back to normalcy and lie among our strewn clothes in each other's arms, waiting for our pulses to quiet. Beneath us, the boat rocks gently, rhythmically, and I listen to the slap slap slap of the water against the hull. In the trough of a wave, I glimpse a gull sitting on the water, its profile to us, listening like a cat. I miss my cat, my sweet fat cat. She was jealous of Angie, and Angie was a little jealous of her. Though the cat always slept at the foot of my bed if I was alone in it, she never came near it when Angie was with me. Making love without saying anything not I love you or my darling or your name your name or what she used to murmur against my throat my breast is it really you oh it's really you I've been waiting all my life for you how we felt so together so close so one. Who's your man!

"Why are you crying?" he asks, stroking my arm.

"Am I? Nothing. You know, post-coital tristesse."

"That was so good," he says, "so really good. Why didn't you say it?"

"That you're my man?"

"Yeah."

"Because you're not my man."

"Who is?"

"Nobody. Nobody's my man."

He sighs. "You and me, Annie. You know, I think we could make it together."

"Don't say anything, Artie," I say. "I'm nowhere near ready for anything like that."

"What are you ready for?"

"The rest of my lunch."

TWENTY (Now)

In the morning, I awaken to my mother's voice. She is shouting, "Max, Max, *Max.*" I run down the hall to their bedroom.

"What is it?" I ask, frightened. She's in her night-gown, standing next to his bed.

"I don't know. He won't wake up. His breathing is wrong."

"I'll call the rescue squad." I lunge for the phone, the number I want so urgently conspicuous, big and bright red, pasted to the phone on the night table. A voice answers at once and I give it the information it needs and hang up. My father's breaths are a long rattle in his throat. Death rattle, I think, and I see on his face a look of intense concentration, as though behind the closed lids his eyes are trying to pene-trate some murky dark. He is working hard to master some-thing, or to remember, and then I see him come half up out of bed to reach for a breath and not get it, and I know that what he was striving for was to keep his life in his body, and that he has failed.

"He's stopped," I say. The breathing has stopped, but what I really mean is that he has stopped.

"Do you think so?" my mother says in a peculiar, small voice, as though death is a matter of opinion.

"He's dead."

"How can he be dead?" She shakes his shoulder and says his name again. "It's impossible. How can Max be dead?"

I don't believe it either. This is the first time I've seen anyone die, and he is my father. This is Caesar. I touch his arm and feel the closeness of the bone. How frail, this man who was always a bull. I never really believed he was mortal. (Ah, then I am mortal, too). How incredible, all that life, that power, energy, vitality, the rage, the huge voice, the appetite, the arrogance and self-love, all of it has stopped. I'm suffused by awe, reduced by it, then swollen with pity. Pity for my father! How he feared his death, and now he has had it. The tenses have shifted. Max Silver, my father, was, he had, he did, he used to. All he is now is dead.

My mother is weeping softly. I get her robe and put it around her shaking shoulders, and find that I'm crying, too. "Come into the kitchen," I say. "I'll make coffee."

"He can't be dead," she says in that strange small voice as I lead her away. "We've been married almost sixty years."

She sits at the kitchen table, weeping into a Kleenex, while I fiddle with her complicated electric percolator, my hands trembling. How natural and simple death is, finally. I think of that younger version of me, the one I have so much trouble feeling was really me, early in my marriage, when we were still living in the castle and I was falling apart, panicked and obsessed by the thought of dying. I am confused by time's gift of calm acceptance. Or is it not a gift, but a theft?

"It goes away," Kantfogel said. "And once it goes, it will never come back." I didn't believe him, the panic was so consuming, the fear so intense.

"How can it go away? Death is real. It's really going to happen."

"To fear death is natural, but not this kind of fear. Death is part of life. When you accept your life, you will accept your death."

I didn't know what he was talking about, but all the same, it went away. But this is my father's death. Whatever his life has been, now that it's ended it has its full shape.

As we wait for the rescue squad, I become my father and begin to drown in his life, his life as I remember and imagine it through all the stories and the few photographs. He is the child who never looked like a child, his face already set, by the time of the first photograph, clenched, determined to survive. He is the boy in knickers holding onto the hand of his ugly little brother, Leo, looking strong and broad-shouldered by comparison, ready to fight off all enemies.

But then he's the boy in the grade-school graduation picture, in the bottom row, sitting cross-legged on the floor, one of the smallest, yet the fiercest. He is the bar mitzvah boy in the big picture, on cracked board, with the lock of real hair glued to it by his mother, a rare gesture of love. In none of these photos is he smiling. He doesn't smile as a young man, either, in any of the pictures that exist only in my memory of his stories, not as an adolescent youth being taught by his boss how to eat in restaurants, nor as the young man being taken, again by his boss, to a prostitute, his first woman, hoping while he tests his manhood that there will be enough money left afterwards to go to a Chinese restaurant. He is almost smiling in the newspaper photograph of his departure on the Ile de France for Paris, dressed in spats and Chesterfield and homburg, an important young manufacturer off to see for himself from the fashion masters whether hems will be up or down in the coming season. He doesn't smile at the Louvre, either, when he tells a guide who offers to show him around, "I haven't got time for the whole shmear. Show me your six best numbers." He has rarely had time, and now he has no more time, and I know why I'm crying. He isn't smiling in the photograph with the Pope, to whom he has just said, "This isn't for me, Pope, I'm Jewish. It's for the Italians who work for me. They'll be thrilled to death." I doubt if he smiled much as a young bridegroom, at first shy and scared of the stranger who was his wife, beautiful, more educated than he, then resentful of her because she wanted to spend his money. ("Everybody has carpets on the floor, Max." "Yeah? Well, I'm not everybody!") He never smiles when he comes home at night, tired, aggravated, expecting the worst. I know this at first hand because I am three years old and sitting on the kitchen floor, waiting for him, wondering if he can go through the doorway without stooping to keep from hitting his head, and what a surprise when he comes and there's all that space between his head and the top of the doorframe. Later, I see him smile at customers, buyers, in the showroom, but never in back at the people who work for him. He doesn't begin to smile, really, until long after the depression, and then not until he has retired from the dress business, and then only rarely, and only because he has begun to have a little time, though not much.

All this, his life, his death, in less than ten minutes when I hear the rescue squad thundering down the long outside hallway. I open the kitchen door to let them through.

"In the back," I say, as they fly past me, two men with equipment, a blur of white and aluminum. I follow, leaving my mother huddled at the kitchen table. She knows he's dead, that it's useless, even though she doesn't believe it.

"His heart," I call after the men, "he has a pace-maker." But they know what to do. They know it's his heart. In the end, it's always the heart. When I reach the bedroom door, I see my father's feet bounce up and fall back. Like kicking a stalled machine, they are pounding his chest. I wince, wanting to tell them not to do that, to leave him alone, to stop hurting him. Instead, I go back to the kitchen. My mother is crying into the telephone. "Yes, they're here," she says. "Yes, I will. No. Yes, I have." She hangs up. "The doctor. He has an office full of people, but he's sending Dr. Wishnick right over. He says I should take a Valium."

"I'll get it," I say.

"I don't need a Valium," she says. "Why should I be tranquil at a time like this?"

One of the paramedics, holding a pencil and a printed form, comes into the kitchen.

"Who's his doctor?" he asks in a calm, matter-of-fact voice.

"I just called him. Arthur Greenberg."

"What's his hospital?"

"Hallandale Mount Zion."

"All right. We're taking him there. We'll contact the doctor."

"What for?"

"We've got his breathing going again. It probably doesn't mean anything. Don't get your hopes up."

"He's not dead?"

"He's breathing."

"He's alive?"

"He's breathing," he says, over his shoulder, heading back to the bedroom. "Breathing isn't necessarily alive."

My mother runs after him, with me right behind her.

"But it's not dead, either?" my mother asks.

They're loading him onto a stretcher, tightly wrapped in blankets, tubes in his nostrils reconnecting him to not dead, whatever it is.

"Wait one minute," my mother says. "I'll throw on some clothes and come with you."

"Can't wait," they say, trotting down the hall with my father between them. "He'll be in the intensive care unit."

"I run ahead to open the door for them. They are truly remarkable, these men whose faces I haven't had time to see, these efficient angels of life.

"I don't understand," my mother says a few minutes later, as we descend to the garage in the musical elevator which is playing Deep Purple, a tune from my moody adolescence. "What does science think it's doing? In the old days, except in the bible, if you died you died."

The elevator stops on the tenth floor to admit two elderly women. One of them is Flora.

"Polly!" she screams happily. Then, seeing my mother's face, her own fills with concern.

"Max?" she asks.

My mother nods.

"The rescue squad just took him to the hospital," I explain. "He died, but they got him breathing again." The music soars over our heads, over sleepy garden walls.

"Oh, Polly," Flora wails, clasping my mother's hands. "What can I do? Tell me what I can do. I'll do anything."

"What can anyone do?" my mother asks, shrugging. They are old friends. "Try praying."

"I'll pray," Flora says. "I'm praying now. I'll pray till the cows come home."

.   .   .

An eye slowly, tentatively opens, testing, then quickly shuts again; but in that brief moment what was revealed was alive and incredibly blue. Vikings overran Eastern Europe and stayed long enough to leave blue for my father's eyes, and for mine, and red for my grandfather's hair. I've been sitting at his bedside watching him for the past hour, listening to his improved breathing, trying not to think of a chloroformed frog whose interior I once laid bare for a science experiment. I kept the frog's heart beating with a slow drip of salt water, and, though technically alive, that frog was beyond ever again seeing anything.

I ring for a nurse. "He opened an eye," I tell her when she comes. She feels his pulse, then raises one of his eyelids. The eye that looks out at her is neither rolled up in its socket, nor blind. It is, as I've already noted, much bluer than I remember it ever having been, perhaps because of his pallor. It's also as fierce as a hawk's. His voice now rumbles up out of his chest.

"Take it awaaaaay," he commands, and the nurse, turning to smile at me, lets his eyelid close. "Take itawaaaaay," he nonetheless repeats, in a somewhat stronger voice. "Take it AWAAAY."

"I'll get the doctor," the nurse says, trotting off. My father's eyes slowly open again, both of them. He stares at me.

"Where's Polly?" he asks. "Where's my WIFE?"

"She's right down the hall," I say, rising. "I'll get her."

She's in the waiting room. Waiting. And smoking. It's been a long vigil. She looks up at me, expecting the worst. I smile.

"He's awake. Talking. He wants you."

A strange mixture of feelings crosses her face, fear predominating. There is something terrible about recalling the dead; where have they been and what of that place will they bring back with them?

"Well, he's not a vegetable," I say, as we hurry into the room. "That's certain."

His eyes are open when we come in, darting back and forth. Plugged into all this machinery, he can't move.

"Where the hell were you?" he asks angrily, accusingly. I half expect him to go on. I died, and what were you doing, smoking cigarettes, doing puzzles?

"I was right here," she tells him defensively, a posture she may have been expecting never to resume.

"You were not here. Don't tell me you were here. Where was I?"

She looks at him blankly, holding her tongue.

"You were right here, too," I say.

"I was not here. Don't tell me I was here. Get me out of here." He begins to cry. My mother moves to pat his hands, but the veins on both of them are wired.

"Shhh, Max," she says, beginning to cry, too. "It's all right."

"Don't tell me it's all right," he growls. Where has he found the strength for all this anger? "Don't tell me it's

- 223 -

all right. I know it's not all right. I want to go to the kitchen."

"You can't go to the kitchen, Max," my mother says. "We're not home. We're in the hospital."

"Don't tell me I'm in the hospital. I'm not in any Goddamn hospital. I know where I am. Don't you think I know where I am?" His face is contorted with rage. His voice is the snarl of an animal. A young doctor hurries in, breathless, a stethoscope waving against his chest.

"How's the patient feeling now?" The doctor gropes for my father's pulse.

"Oh, doctor," my father says.

"You're doing fine, Mr. Silver. "There was a little problem but we've got it straightened out now."

He snaps the stethoscope into his ears and listens to my father's heart. "Good," he says. "Very good. How do you feel?"

"Tired, doctor. Boy am I tired. Soooo tired. I am fatigued, exhausted, dead, you wouldn't believe how tired I am, doctor." His voice sounds unnatural, as if he is sending it into the air, a trial balloon, listening to it himself, to the sound of it and for the meaning of the words. He is orating, his head slightly cocked. "Tired, tired, tired. I am OVERWHELMED with tired."

"Well, you can rest now," the doctor says. "Sleep. You'll get stronger. You're a very lucky man, Mr. Silver."

Going home, propped up on the backseat of the car between my mother and the day nurse, he talks ceaselessly.

"I am a lucky man. The doctor says I am a very lucky man. I kiss that doctor. I kiss all the doctors. The young doctor, and the old doctor, and Dr. Greenberg and the nurses, the white nurses and the black nurses and the in-between nurses. I kiss the rescue squad. Oh what a lucky man I am, a lucky lucky lucky lucky man oh boy am I a lucky man." He is chanting, his voice now too large for his body. "Lucky lucky lucky lucky." I nearly smash the car into the one ahead of me.

"That's all we'd need now," my mother says.

.   .   .

He's at his desk, the nurse hovering behind his chair. He is silent, staring into a ledger. He has been staring, his face expressionless, for almost an hour. There's something he needs to know, but he can't recall what it is. I come over to see if I can help him. The ledger is upside down.

The brain scan shows that one hemisphere of his brain is completely dead. He has lost the most important thing in his world: numbers.

.   .   .

He's in the bedroom in the rented hospital bed with the crib sides. "I am a lucky man. I am full of joy. I am overcome with joy. I am drunk with joy. I am consumed with joy." Where has he found all these words, some I can't recall his ever having used before? Fascinated, I've been sitting here for hours, listening to him. He slips from abusive rage to this uncharacteristic declaiming in this uncharacteristic vocabulary. It's as if thought and voice are one, speech nonvolitional. Clearly, he is listening to the sound of his own voice, repeating and repeating, but altering the vocal nuances. "Where am I? Home? I am home in my darling home with the ceilings. Who needs all these ceilings? Yards and yards of ceilings, wall-to-wall ceilings. It's a good thing I don't have to carpet them. Too much ceiling, much too much ceiling."

The nurse comes in to interrupt him with a handful of pills and a glass of water. Dutifully, one by one, he swallows the pills. The nurse encourages him with little clucks of approval, as though he is a good and obedient child. He gives her a false, childlike smile. "Do you like this face?" he asks, grimacing sweetly. "This is a good face. A very goooood face. I want soup. I want six, eight, ten plates of soup. I want to GOUGE myself on soup. Gouge? Is that a good word? Do I have any money left? My mother used to make soup, boy did she make soup, she made luckshen, farfel, borscht, schav, she was a regular machine, a soup machine, her middle name was soup, she was the mother souperior, ha, ha, ha. When I went into business that first year working all day and all night she would come to the Place with a big jar of hot soup, I should only live and succeed, she'd have followed me all over the world with her soup, the only love she ever gave me was soup, with a can opener you can get all the love you need now. No, take it away, I cannot eat, I cannot EAT. Take it away, take it awaaaay, take it AWAAAAY."

Some time during the night, he stops talking and dies. The nurse assumes that he has at last fallen asleep and my mother and I, relieved that there is at last silence, fall into our own restless sleep. In the morning, when the nurse comes in to tell us he is dead, we know that this time he is really dead. I spend a long time wondering why it was given to him, like a Jewish curse, to die twice.

TWENTY-ONE (Now)

"That rabbi!" Flora says. "A golden tongue. There wasn't a dry seat in the house."

There is a moment of absolute silence before Jed and I collapse in laughter, and soon everyone follows except Flora, who looks bewildered. What a relief! It's true, almost everyone at the funeral service was weeping, though not necessarily for my father. They're all survivors with their own dead to remember and mourn, though it was my father so still and silent in the coffin, with the morning sun slanting dramatically through the chapel's tall windows behind him, behind the rabbi with the golden tongue. Lighting courtesy of God, the rabbi's eulogy courtesy of his short pre-service conversation with my mother and me, when we told him what we could. Like the rabbi at my wedding so long ago, this one is a stranger. And, though he was a stranger, extolling my father's virtues as we had just haltingly described them to him, the cantor's voice was strong and true and moving, and the Hebrew prayers, the Kaddish, echoing through five thousand years of sorrow and mourning, gave dignity to this, my father's final ritual.

Tomorrow we fly to New York to bury him in the family plot where, he once assured me, there will be a place for me, too, now that I have nowhere better to go.

There is a moment during the close of the funeral service when, just before the coffin is closed and the lid screwed down, the family comes forward for a last look at "the departed." It's an emotional moment, full of finality, the reality of forever, equaled only by the moment when, the coffin lowered into the grave and the first spadeful of earth thrown upon it, one turns to walk away, back into one's own life. The solitariness of the dead. We stood and looked into the coffin at the familiar face and wept our silent goodbyes. I held my mother's hand and Jed held mine in his huge, warm, gentle one, comforting me with continuity, so that the moment filled with a complex wash of feelings. I was grateful for Jed's grown-up, loving presence, glad in a way I'd never before been to have been a link in this chain of life. I was also aware of my mother, who wept as though her heart was irrevocably broken, and it came to me that dead tyrants leave empty spaces as large as anyone's, perhaps even larger. And I wept for my father, as I wept in the moments of his first, aborted death, trying to think only of him and to think kindly, but the hands folded across his breast were my hands, and the eyes beneath the sealed lids were my eyes. Goodbye, goodbye.

And somewhere, deep and almost out of range of conscious thought, it was time for Angie to die, and I said goodbye to her, too. No more au revoir. Goodbye, goodbye.

"So what did I say?" Flora wails, looking from one to the other of us. "Did I say something wrong?"

"You never say anything exactly wrong," Tina Sperber tells her, but she is laughing too hard to go on. There's a lot of movement in the room; the women are bustling about, carrying trays from the kitchen laden with funeral meats, delicatessen, bread, Danish pastry, dishes and cutlery, setting up the buffet.

"So tell me why is it," Flora says, "that all I have to do is open my mouth, and ninety-nine times out of ten everyone laughs." As they now do again, even my mother. "Why?" she pleads. "Will someone tell me why?"

The men, except for Jed, aren't helping with the buffet. They're sitting in the card nook, smoking cigars and looking solemn. Artie is one of them. He sees me coming out with the big coffee urn and jumps up to help.

"What do you say I come with you to New York tomorrow?" he says, taking the urn from me. "Where do you want this?" I show him, and he puts it down and bends to plug it in.

"It's just the immediate family," I say. "But it's sweet of you to offer."

"No, I mean it, I'd really like to come."

"Thanks Artie, but no." I don't want him there. My mother and I will stay in New York for a few days and when I've seen her off on her plane, I'm going to stay on a little longer and look for an apartment. It's time to come home.

"You won't believe this," Artie says, following me into the kitchen, "but I'm starved." He grins at me. "There's nothing like a funeral to perk up the appetite."

All the appetites, I think, feeling not only hungry but sexy. I'm so glad to have my body. I almost tell Artie that I wish we could go somewhere and make love, but no, he would take it personally. I see my mother watching us from above her handkerchief, so pleased that I've made this conquest. I wonder, as I have before, whether she knew the truth about Angie, if she let herself know, because I can't believe that anyone who really knew me or cared about me, could have failed to know. Maybe that's why she's so pleased about Artie. Is it that I'm not a total freak, that I'm back in the fold, or is it simply that if I marry there will be someone to care about me and to take care of me?

I'm not back in the fold.

It's a very long day, but like all the days, the sun finally sets on it, the mourners depart, and my mother, exhausted, goes to bed. Jed and I go out on the balcony, where the air smells of sea and of impending rain. There is no moon and the sea is a darker, noisier dark, a restless presence. We lean on the concrete rail and look out and talk of Nick, sorry that he couldn't be here, that we couldn't locate him in time. He is probably sitting in some desert, stoned on something.

"Don't worry about him, Mom," Jed says. "He'll come out of it. Underneath all this, he's really very square and sentimental."

"Tell me about Susan," I say, and he does. He thinks he's in love with her. She makes him feel good about himself, and he does the same for her. "I think that's love. Is it?"

I think how rotten Angie and I made each other feel those last years, and yet I loved her. "I don't know," I say. "It's not a very selfless love, is it?" I remember Santha, that spring, saying, "There are three levels of love. In the first, the lover thinks: what can my lover give me? In the second, the lover thinks: what can my lover and I give each other? But in the third, the highest level, the lover thinks only: what can I give to my beloved? I tell this to Jed.

"I'm not a Hindu," he says. "I haven't learned to live without my ego." Neither, I think, have I.

We're silent for a while, then he asks, "Do you ever see Angie, Mom?"

"No. Not for almost two years. I don't even know where she is."

"Do you miss her?"

"Yes, but I'm going to stop."

"Can you just decide?"

"I don't know. I'll see."

The sea sighs around us. I feel a rush of love for Jed, recalling how I adored him when he was that spidery, charming baby, and how much I missed that little boy when he vanished, swallowed by this large, competent, untempestuous young man. I love this young man, too, though he is someone else. As I am. As I have been.

"Life is strange," he says. "When I was little, I never doubted that the one constant in life was my family. We all seemed so locked into each other. In a good way. Now Dad's with Marilyn, Nick's God knows where, and you . . . " His voice trails off.

And me? He doesn't know, and neither do I. I listen to the pulse of the sea, feeling very small.

"Tell me, Mom," he says. "If you had it to do over again . . ."

"Would I live my life the same way?"

What a question!

About the Author

Edith Konecky has lived most of her life in New York City except for some years as a suburban housewife and mother of two sons. She is currently at work on a new novel tentatively titled *Fiction and the Facts of Life*.

CPSIA information can be obtained
at www.ICGtesting.com
Printed in the USA
BVHW070227261218
536360BV00001B/31/P